Sinking
– the –
Dayspring

Trailblazer Books

Gladys Aylward • *Flight of the Fugitives*
Mary McLeod Bethune • *Defeat of the Ghost Riders*
William & Catherine Booth • *Kidnapped by River Rats*
Charles Loring Brace • *Roundup of the Street Rovers*
Governor William Bradford • *The Mayflower Secret*
John Bunyan • *Traitor in the Tower*
Amy Carmichael • *The Hidden Jewel**
Peter Cartwright • *Abandoned on the Wild Frontier*
George Washington Carver • *The Forty-Acre Swindle*
Elizabeth Fry • *The Thieves of Tyburn Square*
Jonathan & Rosalind Goforth • *Mask of the Wolf Boy*
Barbrooke Grubb • *Ambushed in Jaguar Swamp*
Sheldon Jackson • *The Gold Miners' Rescue*
Adoniram & Ann Judson • *Imprisoned in the Golden City*
Festo Kivengere • *Assassins in the Cathedral*
David Livingstone • *Escape From the Slave Traders**
Martin Luther • *Spy for the Night Riders**
Dwight L. Moody • *Danger on the Flying Trapeze*
Lottie Moon • *Drawn by a China Moon*
Samuel Morris • *Quest for the Lost Prince*
George Müller • *The Bandit of Ashley Downs*
John Newton • *The Runaway's Revenge*
Florence Nightingale • *The Drummer Boy's Battle*
John G. Paton • *Sinking the Dayspring*
William Penn • *Hostage on the Nighthawk*
Joy Ridderhof • *Race for the Record*
Nate Saint • *The Fate of the Yellow Woodbee*
William Seymour • *Journey to the End of the Earth*
Menno Simons • *The Betrayer's Fortune*
Mary Slessor • *Trial by Poison*
Hudson Taylor • *Shanghaied to China**
Harriet Tubman • *Listen for the Whippoorwill*
William Tyndale • *The Queen's Smuggler*
John Wesley • *The Chimney Sweep's Ransom*
Marcus & Narcissa Whitman • *Attack in the Rye Grass*
David Zeisberger • *The Warrior's Challenge*

*Hero Tales: A Family Treasury of True Stories
From the Lives of Christian Heroes* (Volumes I, II, III, & IV)

*Curriculum guide available.
Written by Julia Pferdehirt with Dave & Neta Jackson.   01C

Sinking
– the –
Dayspring

Dave & Neta Jackson

Illustrated by Anne Gavitt

BETHANY HOUSE PUBLISHERS
MINNEAPOLIS, MINNESOTA 55438

Published by Bethany House Publishers
A Ministry of Bethany Fellowship International
11400 Hampshire Avenue South
Bloomington, Minnesota 55438
www.bethanyhouse.com

Printed in the United States of America by
Bethany Press International, Bloomington, Minnesota 55438

Library of Congress Cataloging-in-Publication Data

Jackson, Dave.
    Sinking the Dayspring : John G. Paton / by Dave & Neta Jackson ;
text illustrations by Anne Gavitt.
        p.   cm. — (Trailblazer books)
    "The experiences of missionary John G. Paton, Captain Fraser, and
the Dayspring are true except for a few details."—T.p. verso.
    Summary: In 1866, a fourteen-year-old orphan reluctantly joins the
crew of a missionary ship leaving Australia, but when a hurricane
strands him on a South Sea island and he is captured by slave traders,
he finds the courage to trust in God.
        ISBN 0–7642–2268–6 (pbk.)
    1. Paton, John Gibson, 1824–1907—Juvenile fiction. 2. Missions—
Vanuatu—Juvenile fiction. [1. Paton, John Gibson, 1824–1907—
Fiction. 2. Missionaries—Fiction. 3. Missions—Vanuatu—Fiction.
4. Slave trade—Fiction. 5. Christian life—Fiction. 6. Orphans—
Fiction. 7. Islands of the Pacific—Fiction.] I. Jackson, Neta.
II. Gavitt, Anne, ill. III. Title.
PZ7.J132418 Shc 2001
[Fic]   dc21   2001002772

The South Sea Islands known now as Vanuatu were called the New Hebrides at the time of this story.

Although thousands of children and adults in Australia and Scotland purchased "shares" to help build the missionary ship *Dayspring*, Kevin Gilmore is fictional.

On the other hand, the experiences of missionary John G. Paton, Captain Fraser, and the *Dayspring* are true except for a few details and the following facts.

The hurricane that first wrecked the *Dayspring* occurred on January 6, 1873—several years later than 1866, as implied by this story. The second storm that finally broke her back had no known human assistance. It was simply strong enough to drag the ship's anchor until she smashed into the coral reef.

Paton does not name the trading ship or slave traders who took over the *Dayspring*. However, for the sake of the story, we borrowed names from a typical incident in 1884 when HMS *Swinger* intercepted the *Hopeful* and arrested Agent McNeil and Boatswain Williams as notorious slave traders in the region.

Find us on the Web at . . .

TrailblazerBooks.com

- Meet the authors.

- Read the first chapter of each book—
  with the pictures.

- Track the Trailblazers around the world
  on a map.

- Use the historical timeline to find out
  what other important events were happening in the world at the time of each
  Trailblazer story.

- Discover how the authors research their
  books and link to some of the same
  sources they used where
  you can learn more
  about these heroes.

- Write to the authors.

- Explore frequently asked
  questions about writing
  and Trailblazer books.

Just point your browser to *www.trailblazerbooks.com*

CONTENTS

DAVE AND NETA JACKSON are a full-time husband/wife writing team who have authored and coauthored many books on marriage and family, the church, relationships, and other subjects. Their books for children include the TRAILBLAZER series and *Hero Tales,* volumes I, II, III, and IV. The Jacksons make their home in Evanston, Illinois.

Chapter 1

Ship Shares

The few cents Kevin Gilmore earned picking up chips and throwing them into the bin at the end of the ferry dock wouldn't buy him a sweet cake. He had to take the money home to help his mother pay their rent.

He removed his hat and wiped the sweat from his forehead. If only he could get a real job hauling firewood for the paddle-wheel steamer, he could make a difference. But the older boys got those jobs.

Two of them swaggered toward him. "Hey, Gilmore, pick up those scraps before I trip over 'em." The larger boy pretended to stumble and staggered toward Kevin. Kevin tried to dodge out of his way, but

the older boy bumped him with his shoulder and pushed him off the dock and into the water.

Kevin panicked as he fell. He couldn't swim! Then, *splash*! The water closed over him, and everything seemed to happen in slow motion. Thousands of glimmering silver bubbles rose toward the bright green above while he sank into the dark. He was going to die. He was certain of it. He had always been afraid of drowning, and now it was happening to him.

He slashed at the water with his hands, clawing, grabbing, trying to climb back up to the surface. How did people swim? If he'd only learned. Then suddenly, without knowing how he'd managed it, he burst from the water, sputtering and yelling for help. He reached toward the dock, but his head went under again, filling his mouth and lungs with salt water.

He bobbed up again, choking and gasping for breath. He was drowning. He knew it. He couldn't get his breath.

His hand struck something sharp as he swung his arms around. It stung, but it had been solid. Kevin turned his body and grabbed. It was the piling for the dock, covered with sharp barnacles. He pulled himself to the wooden post, clinging so tightly that blood oozed from both hands where the sharp shells cut his fingers.

From above came a roar of laughter.

Kevin looked up into the faces of the boys who had pushed him off the dock. "You want a rope?" one of them called.

Still coughing out seawater, he nodded.

Moments later a thick rope dangled by his side. Then he heard the boys running up the dock. Kevin grasped the rope and painfully pulled himself hand over hand as he "walked" up the piling. He clambered onto the dock and lay there like a pile of seaweed.

When he caught his breath and opened his eyes, a pair of rough boots were before his face. He looked up and saw the dock boss.

"Whatcha think you're doin'? I didn't hire you to go swimming. Look at this dock. It's still covered with chips. You're fired!"

"But, sir, I didn't go swimming. I can't swim. I was pu— I fell in by accident." As much as he hated the bullies who had given him the dunking, it wouldn't do to tell on them. They'd just get back at him some other way.

"If you're that clumsy, you don't belong on the docks. Now get out of here!"

Kevin walked up the pier, squishing with each step and draining water from his clothes like a leaky bucket. At the end, he climbed onto some large rocks and sat there with his head in his hands.

He didn't know how long he had been there letting the bright Australian sunshine warm him, when he looked out into Sydney Cove and saw a sleek new ship slowly creeping into the harbor. It was a two-masted, sharp-bowed brigantine about a hundred feet long. Kevin watched in admiration as its white sails, flapping in the light breeze, were lowered and furled to the booms and yards.

He feared the water, but he sure loved watching ships when his feet were solidly anchored on land. And this was a particularly graceful ship. He strained to see its name—*Dayspring. Dayspring?* He and his mother had once bought shares to help build a ship by that name. Buying shares made them part owners of the ship. At least that's what the missionary had promised.

That was two years ago, when missionary John G. Paton came to their church just after escaping the dangerous cannibals of the South Sea Islands. But he wanted to go back and needed a ship. Kevin had almost forgotten. The missionary had come soon after Kevin's father had been killed in a logging accident. It had been a rough time for Kevin and his mother, but the special mission services had lifted their spirits.

"What we need," said the missionary, "is a missionary ship that can go from island to island taking supplies to the missionaries, encouraging them . . . and rescuing them if necessary." He held up some beautiful certificates. "I have here in my hand genuine shares in the new ship we will name the *Dayspring.* You can purchase these shares today and be part owner in this great work of God. Who wants to be first, just six cents each?"

Many of the children went forward to buy three or four, even ten certificates. But Kevin's mother had handed him enough money to buy a hundred shares. Being as poor as they were, he was shocked, but his mother reassured him. "Don't worry. God will care for us." So Kevin took the money forward and proudly returned with a stack of shares as thick as a small book. They looked almost like money with a beautifully engraved picture of a sailing ship printed on them and the words *This certificate entitles you to one share ownership in the missionary ship* Dayspring. Across the bottom of the certificate Kevin read, *You are helping bring the Gospel to those who have never heard.*

Since then Kevin had nearly forgotten about the shares. Where had his mother stored them? He'd have to ask her when he got home. He stood up as the new ship's anchor splashed into the bay. Could this be the same *Dayspring* in which he and his mother held part ownership?

✧ ✧ ✧ ✧

An hour later when the *Dayspring*'s longboat nosed into the pier, Kevin was there to take the rope and tie it up. But his hopes that this was "his" *Dayspring* were already fading. The six sailors rowing the boat were arguing loudly with the seventh man—obviously the captain—sitting in the back at the tiller.

"If we don't get paid, we're not hoisting another sail on that ship!"

"Don't tell *us* what your problems are, Cap'n! This is 1865—maritime laws require you to pay us!"

"Sell the ship if need be, but pay us our money.

We want it now!"

The sailors climbed out of the boat and walked up the pier without so much as giving Kevin a glance.

The fourteen-year-old boy headed home. His mother had been very sick lately—too sick to work, was his opinion. But she forced herself to continue doing the heavy laundry of Sydney's rich people. He shook his head. If his mother hadn't spent all that money on shares in the *Dayspring*, they would have a little extra now so that she could rest and get well. But now their money was gone with nothing to show for it but some fancy pieces of paper.

As Kevin pushed open the door, he saw his mother lying on her bed, shivering in the heat of January, which was summer in Australia. "You don't look good, Mama. Are you feelin' real bad?"

"I . . . I'll be all right. Just got dizzy standing over those hot tubs. But I've got to get up and finish. If I don't have those sheets back to the hotel by morning, I'm liable to lose my job." She tried to sit up.

"No, no," Kevin said. "You rest. I'll finish the sheets."

She fell back onto the bed. "You can't lift those big heavy things."

But Kevin was out of the house before she could stop him. They rented a one-room apartment at the back of McPherson's Emporium. In the small yard off their porch Mrs. Gilmore set up her laundry tubs, built a fire to heat the water, and hung up the clean laundry on lines strung between the porch and the back fence.

Kevin went to work stoking the fire and stirring the tubs with a wooden paddle, but when it came to lifting out the heavy, wet sheets, he had to admit that his mother had been *almost* right. The sheets were heavy, but he managed to get them rinsed and hung on the lines before dark. He went back inside and tried to make some soup while his mother slept. He found a few carrots and turnips and onions, but they were almost out of food.

He set the hot soup beside her bed and helped her sit up. "Don't we have any more food?"

Mrs. Gilmore sighed. "Only what you found in the box. I was hoping to get paid for the laundry tomorrow and buy more, but Mr. McPherson came asking for the rent this morning. It's late, so I guess we have to pay him first."

Kevin's eyes darkened. "We never should have bought those shares."

"Shares? What shares? What are you talking about, son?"

"You know, for that ship."

His mother shook her head and took another spoon of soup.

"You know. The missionary who came to church a couple years ago wanting us to buy shares to build a missionary ship."

"Oh yes. Rev. John Paton." Mrs. Gilmore leaned her head back and with a smile gazed up as though she were seeing a vision of the ship. "We bought a hundred, didn't we?"

"Yeah. Where are they, Mama?"

"I don't know. I put them in that waterproof pouch of your father's, but I have no idea where it is now."

The next day Kevin delivered the hotel laundry and paid Mr. McPherson. He stayed home the next day, too, to help his mother, but she didn't seem to be getting better. She needed rest, and she needed more food. Kevin felt desperate.

On the third day, his mother claimed that she was strong enough to do the laundry by herself. "Go on down to the docks and see if you can get some work. I'll be all right." But she didn't look any better to Kevin. Still, they needed more money—fast.

At the docks along Sydney Cove, the boss spotted Kevin and yelled, "Where have you been? Look at that ferry dock. It's covered with scraps. You think I'm going to break my back picking all that up? I've a good mind to fire you for not showing up for work."

"Uh, you did fire me, sir."

"What?"

"I said, you fired me the other day after those . . . after I fell in the water."

"Why would I do that? Get to work, and be quick about it. We haven't got all day."

Kevin set to work as fast as he could, all the time watching the boss out of the corner of his eye. A man that unpredictable might do anything. Kevin stood up to catch his breath and looked at the boss telling some workmen where to stack some barrels. If he was in a good mood, maybe Kevin could ask him for the pay he'd earned the other day before he was "fired." On the other hand, bringing it up might get him fired again.

Kevin went back to picking up the wood chips and pieces of bark.

Shortly after noon, he noticed the captain of the new ship walking along the dock talking to a man with a short, sharply trimmed beard. The man looked familiar . . . Kevin stared. It was the missionary, the one who had sold shares to build a ship! Kevin looked back out at the ship in the bay. *Dayspring* . . . it must be the mission ship, the one he and his mom helped build. That was his ship out there!

Kevin dropped his armload of chips and headed up the pier toward the two men. He rubbed his hands together. He'd tell 'em he helped build their ship. The missionary said buying shares made them part owners. He hurried his pace to catch up with the men.

"Hey, where do you think you are going?"

Kevin turned back to see the dock boss with his hands on his hips.

"You better get back here right now, or you'll forfeit *all* your pay."

Kevin looked at the men walking away, then back at the boss. He thought of his mother and wiped his arm across his forehead. He had to get paid. Reluctantly he turned around and went back to picking up chips. But all the rest of that afternoon he kept glancing at the *Dayspring* and thinking about his shares in the ship.

Ship owners were rich men. So how could shareholders in a ship that beautiful be in danger of starving like he and his mom were? It didn't make sense. Maybe they shouldn't have given their money. His mother had said God would take care of them, but now look at them.

Slowly an idea began to form in Kevin's mind. Maybe he had a solution. Maybe those shares would help him and his mom now that they were in such great need. He worked faster. He wanted to get finished and go check out his idea before the *Dayspring* sailed, before he was too late.

Chapter 2

The Owner's Request

When Kevin got home late that afternoon, he was glad to see the laundry hanging on the lines, but inside he found his mom flopped across her bed as though she had passed out before she could even swing her feet up to make herself more comfortable. Her mouth hung open, and she breathed with exhausted sighs. He didn't dare wake her, so he moved quietly as he began searching their one-room apartment for the *Dayspring* shares. He was sure they would solve their problems . . . at least for a time.

He looked in boxes and bags without success, then noticed his mother's large family Bible on the shelf. Of course! They bought the shares at church. She would have naturally put them in the old Bible. He got it down, sat on the chair by the window, and opened it.

He quickly flipped through the pages. He couldn't miss them, not a stack of one hundred. But they weren't there. Instead, he came across the family history pages. He knew only a little of his family's history, just that both his parents had come to Australia as prison convicts—like most Australians. Carefully he read what his mother had written.

Isaac Gilmore, born Glasgow, Scotland, 1829. Worked as an apprentice weaver until he was convicted for stealing a pair of geese. He was sentenced to fifteen years in New South Wales and transported in 1849 aboard the Havering.

Mary Healy, born Gloucestershire, England, 1830. While employed as a maid she was convicted of stealing a shawl and other wearing apparel. She was sentenced to seven years on Van Diemen's Land [Tasmania] and transported aboard the Kinnear *in 1848. In less than a year she was transferred to New South Wales.*

Isaac Gilmore and Mary Healy met in Sydney, Australia, and were married November 13, 1849, in the Chalmers Presbyterian Church.

Kevin Gilmore, born February 3, 1851.

Wow! Kevin had never heard all those details. He knew his parents had been convicts, but to think that his father had only stolen a couple geese and his mother had taken a shawl and some other clothes. Kevin didn't want to live in either Scotland or England, but were his grandparents alive? Did he have aunts, uncles, and cousins? He wished he knew.

He closed the Bible and put it back. Now with his father dead and his mother ill, he couldn't look to relatives for help. There was only one opportunity: the ship's shares.

They had to be somewhere.

Under his mother's bed he found a box and quietly pulled it out so as not to awaken her. It contained two quilts and some scraps of cloth, maybe for another quilt, but no packet of shares. As he was pushing the box back under the old iron bed, Kevin noticed a small carpetbag pushed back against the wall. He crawled under and retrieved it.

Inside was a flat waterproof pouch with a long leather thong. His father used to put the thong around his neck and carry the pouch on his chest. Eagerly, Kevin opened the pouch: There were the shares for the *Dayspring*. He took them to the chair by the window and counted them. One hundred shares, each with an engraving of a ship that looked something like the one in the bay and the words: *This certificate entitles you to one share ownership in the missionary ship* Dayspring.

He gripped the shares in his hand and shook them in front of his face. "We are not broke," he whispered fiercely. "The owners of such a fine ship can't be poor!"

Kevin put the shares back into the pouch and hung it around his neck. His mother might not agree with his plan, but he had to do something. He tucked the pouch inside his shirt and kicked the old carpet-bag under the bed. Tonight he would make his mother more soup. Tomorrow he would take care of business.

✧ ✧ ✧ ✧

Kevin headed for the docks early, carefully hiding behind the warehouse and then sneaking between a stack of barrels and a dry-docked fishing boat to stay out of sight of the dock boss. He didn't want to be picking up sticks when his opportunity came.

The wait was worth it. Finally the captain of the *Dayspring* and the missionary came walking along together.

"Excuse me, sirs." Kevin trotted up and began walking beside them. He pulled out his pouch, opened it, and produced his stack of shares. "Rev. Paton, I'm one of the owners of your ship out there."

The captain frowned, but the missionary reached out his hand as one bushy eyebrow rose and he pursed his lips. He took the shares and flipped through them as though they were a deck of cards. A smile spread across his face as he returned them. "An owner you are, young man, and a proud one, I'm

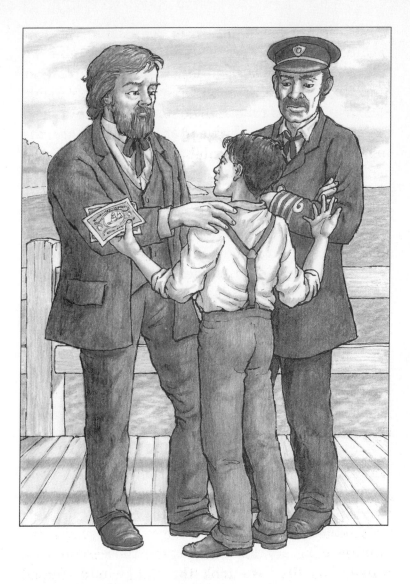

sure. God will bless you for your investment. And as you can see"—he pointed out toward the ship—"we have done just as we said and built a fine ship to help spread the Gospel in the South Sea Islands."

"It is a fine ship," said Kevin, "and I'm glad we were able to help you build it. But, sir, my father died in a logging accident, and my mom's terrible sick. We need to cash in our shares now so we can buy food." He shoved the shares back toward the missionary.

John Paton leaned away from the boy and put up his hand. "I'm sorry, son. There's no way we can buy back those shares. You are, indeed, a part owner, but those shares are not redeemable." By this time all three had arrived at the piling where the *Dayspring*'s longboat was tied up to the dock. Paton shrugged and held out both hands, palms up. "The fact is, we don't have a penny. We couldn't pay you even if we wanted to."

"That's right," put in the captain. "Say, weren't you the boy who helped us tie up our boat the other day?"

"Yes, sir." Kevin thought he hadn't even been noticed.

"Well, then, you saw how upset my crew was. They haven't been paid yet. We have no more money. In fact, they may take us to court and force us to sell the *Dayspring*."

John Paton held up one finger. "Now, hold on a minute, Captain Fraser. I know those men were upset, but they wouldn't do that, would they? I thought we selected good Christian men for this ship. We've got to be careful who we sign on. They are, after all, witnesses for Christ."

The captain crossed his arms and continued as though Kevin weren't standing there. "I'm sure they are fine Christians in terms of their moral behavior. I never had a lick of trouble with them in that regard. But you can't expect men to work for months and sail halfway around the world without pay."

"I know, Captain, but if we don't have it, we don't have it. They can't get something from nothing!"

"But that's their point," said the captain. "They look out there and see a brand-new ship, and they know it's worth a lot of money. Maybe you could just lease it out to some traders for a year or so. That would pay off all your debts and give you some operating money."

"Yes," injected Kevin. "Then you could buy back my shares."

John Paton turned and looked at Kevin. Then he shook his head and put his hand on the boy's shoulder. "I'm sorry. I couldn't do that, son. You see, this ship is dedicated to mission work. Besides," he said, turning to address the captain, "those traders are the last people I'd let touch the *Dayspring*. They are the devil's instruments to destroy the island people. They cheat them. They bring rum and guns. And they oppose all mission work because we're trying to protect the people. Why, did you know that"—John Paton was getting so excited that he was waving his arms and raising his voice—"when I was on the Island of Tanna, one of those traders sent three sailors who had measles into the villages to infect the natives. Of course, measles kills native people because they have no immunity to it. That trader did it on purpose so that—"

"All right, all right." The captain held his hands up in surrender. "We won't lease the ship to any traders, but we've got to pay our crew."

"Of course." John Paton ran his fingers through his hair and took a deep breath. "That's why I asked you to come down here. I want to take the ship down the coast to some of the churches I visited before. When they see that it's actually finished and ready for service, I think they will be willing to contribute additional money." He turned and pointed to the shares that Kevin still held in his hand. "We can sell more shares. I'm sure God will bless. Don't you think you can talk the crew into coming back for a month or so? It shouldn't take long."

The captain shook his head. "I don't know. I might be able to talk a couple of those chaps into coming with us, but the others have families back home. They can't work without pay."

"But if they help us raise some more money, we can pay them. Besides, a couple of men ought to do it. We wouldn't be going far. I'll help sail, and here, here—" He pointed to Kevin. "This boy needs a job. Sign him on. You said yourself that the ship's remarkably easy to sail."

The captain looked at Kevin. "You want a job, boy? You look like a strong lad. Ever been to sea?"

Kevin's mouth dropped open. "No. No, sir. No . . . I couldn't possibly go to sea. I gotta take care of my mother, and . . . and besides . . ." He couldn't bring himself to admit his fear of the water. He didn't know what to say. Then he looked around and saw the dock boss coming his direction with a scowl on his face. "Life aboard ship's just not for me," he mumbled. "This dock is as close to the sea as I ever want to get. Besides, my mom needs me. And right now I better get to work." He turned away, disappointment bowing his head and shoulders. His plan had failed. Even worse, somehow he felt *he* had failed.

✧ ✧ ✧ ✧

When Kevin finished picking up chips late that afternoon and collected his few cents from the dock boss, he headed for home. His head was down and his steps were slow. Sometimes he kicked a pebble ahead of him until it went off to the side. Why go after it? Nothing seemed to be working out. He had hoped that by cashing in the shares for the *Dayspring* he could get enough money to buy food so his mother could rest and recover. Now he was coming home with barely enough money to buy a day's worth of bread.

He really needed to find a better job. He couldn't let his mother keep carrying the heavy load of supporting him. After all, he was almost fourteen, old enough to support her. His mind reviewed his options as he walked: The older boys held the good jobs at the dock. He might try getting a job as a delivery boy for some store, but those jobs were hard to find. He could just take over the laundry that his mom did—maybe he ought to do that. Though if the hotel found out that she wasn't doing it, they might give the work to some other woman.

The last thing he wanted to do was get a job on some sheep station. He knew that would be like disappearing into the wilderness. Men sometimes worked out there for years without ever getting into town. And even then you wouldn't know how to do any other job but herd sheep, so you'd have to go back out there as soon as you ran out of money. No, a sheep station was not for him.

It was dark when he got home, and there was no light in the apartment. Probably his mother was so tired that she fell asleep again before she could fix anything to eat. He went in quietly and lit a candle.

There she was, lying on the bed just like last night. He had hoped to bring her better news, but all he had was the pouch full of certificates and a couple coins for picking up chips.

Kevin looked at his mother again closer. She actually didn't look like she had gotten up from where he'd seen her that morning. He took the candle outside. The laundry was gone, but the tubs and the ground were dry. She hadn't done any washing! He decided that he'd better wake her up.

"Mama." He shook her shoulder gently, then brushed her limp hair from her forehead. "Mama? Mama, wake up."

Mrs. Gilmore turned on her side and moaned.

"Mama, you gotta wake up. I need to ask you something."

Finally she opened her eyes, but they were cloudy, and she had a hard time focusing on his face. "Hi, Kevie."

"Mama, what happened to the laundry? Didn't you do any today?"

"Couldn't. Too sick."

"What happened to the sheets you did yesterday? Did you take them over to the hotel?"

She shook her head, and her eyes drifted closed again.

"Mama. Mama!" But he couldn't rouse her again.

Chapter 3

No Other Choice

All that night Kevin stayed awake beside his mother, wiping her burning hot forehead with a damp cloth. He knew she needed sleep, but he got so scared when she seemed to stop breathing that he shook her shoulder and said softly, "Mama, Mama, don't leave me. Mama, are you still there?"

She moaned and took a reassuring breath. She even moved a little, and Kevin sighed in relief.

The next morning she didn't seem any better, so he ran to Mrs. Hunter's house. She was the head of the Ladies' Aid Society at their church and one of her mother's best friends.

"My mama's real sick," he said. "Could you come and check on her?"

When Mrs. Hunter saw his mother, her eyes grew wide with alarm. "Go get the doctor, Kevin. She needs a doctor."

"But we don't have any money to pay a doctor."

"This isn't the time to talk about money. Just get the doctor as fast as you can."

When the doctor returned with Kevin, he examined her silently, then straightened. "How long has she been like this?"

"I don't know." Kevin bit his lip. "She's been sick a long time, but . . . until yesterday she was still able to do the laundry, though I helped."

"She shouldn't have been working in this condition!" The doctor got out a small bottle and poured some thick, dark liquid into a spoon. Then, lifting Mrs. Gilmore's head a little, he teased the spoon into her mouth and got her to swallow some of the medicine.

He gave the bottle to Mrs. Hunter and said, "I want you to be sure she gets a spoon of this every two or three hours. I'll check back this evening."

For the next two days, Mrs. Hunter nursed Kevin's mother, but late in the night on Wednesday, the sick woman's breathing seemed to stop.

"Is she—?" Kevin couldn't say the word.

Mrs. Hunter put her arm around the boy. Then suddenly his mother took one more breath . . . but it was the last.

After a few moments, Mrs. Hunter pulled the thin blanket up over Mrs. Gilmore's head, and Kevin began to wail. His cries got bigger and bigger, and he felt as though they would never end. It had been bad enough when his father had died, but at least he and his mother had each other. Now to lose his mother, too . . .

After a time he finally seemed to cry himself out, but his breath still came in ragged gulps. It was then that he realized Mrs. Hunter was patting his shoulder and saying, "It's all right, Kevie. It'll be all right. She's with Jesus now."

Suddenly Kevin felt ashamed. He hadn't been thinking about his mother's welfare. He'd been thinking about himself. How could he go on? What would become of him? What would he do? Where would he live?

"Now, you just come on with me over to our house and get something to eat. I'll be sure to send someone to take care of your mother."

✧ ✧ ✧ ✧

Two days later, Kevin's mother was buried beside his father's grave in the old church cemetery. Kevin cried some more—though more quietly this time. When they got back to the Hunters' house, there were three wooden boxes of stuff sitting on the porch.

Mrs. Hunter leaned down and lifted a couple items. "Looks like Mr. McPherson sent your stuff over. That was thoughtful of him."

"Why?" But Kevin knew why. Old Mr. McPherson wasn't going to let someone stay in his apartment without paying. "Didn't even give me a chance," he muttered. "How will I ever find another place to live?" It was the question that had been running around in his head like a dog chasing its tail.

"Now there," said Mrs. Hunter, reaching out for him. But Kevin pulled away. She folded her arms. "Don't you worry, now. You'll be all right here until I can arrange for my brother to pick you up."

"Brother? Who's your brother? What do you mean?"

"My brother Philip. I suppose you could call him Uncle Philip if you want to."

Kevin pressed his lips in a thin line. He wasn't about to call a complete stranger "uncle."

"He runs a huge sheep station," continued Mrs. Hunter. "He always needs help. And I'm sure he'll be glad to make a place for you."

"Herding sheep?"

To Kevin, that sounded like a sentence worse than death. Once a person got stuck out in the wilderness, he might never return. If you were lucky enough not to die of thirst, a poisonous snake might bite you, or you could stumble into a swamp and be eaten by a crocodile. Being sent to a sheep station felt a lot like what had happened to his parents when they had been "transported" to Australia. He couldn't let that happen!

He kneeled down and pawed through the boxes until he found his jacket and hat, another shirt, and the pouch of shares for the *Dayspring*.

"What's that?" asked Mrs. Hunter.

"An old pouch my dad used to carry important papers in." Kevin put it around his neck, bundled his clothes under his arm, and said, "Thank you for everything, Mrs. Hunter. You've been very kind, but I won't be going to a sheep station."

He turned and went down the porch steps.

"Wait! Where are you going? Kevie . . . Kevin, you come back here!"

But by then he was out the gate, walking rapidly down the street. He was ready to run if she tried to follow him, but she stopped at the gate, leaning over it and waving her hand for him to return. "Kevin Gilmore, you come back here right this instant. What do you think you're doing?"

❖ ❖ ❖ ❖

After sleeping in the hayloft of a livery stable for several nights, Kevin began to wonder whether he had made a mistake running away from Mrs. Hunter's. Maybe he should have talked to her and explained how much he did not want to go to the sheep station. Maybe she would have listened to him and let him stay with her.

He looked for a regular job that would pay him enough to rent a room somewhere, but the only employer he knew was the dock boss. Kevin was lucky to get a few hours of work from him picking up chips. He barely earned enough money to buy food.

"If you want a better job from me," growled the dock boss, "then you'll have to prove to me that you're worth it. And you don't do that by skippin' out on me when I give you an assignment. Understand?"

Kevin understood, but he still had a problem: surviving on the streets of Sydney.

He had heard—though he didn't know whether it

was true—that the city officials wouldn't tolerate homeless waifs running the streets of Sydney. Any child who didn't have a family or a home was soon sent off to a sheep station just like Mrs. Hunter had planned to do. Supposedly it was a carry-over from transporting thousands of Britain's "riffraff" to Australia. Here the farmers need workers, so why wait until homeless people turned to petty crime? Just send them where they were needed.

True or not, the fear kept Kevin on edge. He avoided any policemen who might see that he was homeless. It made him feel like he was a criminal even though he hadn't done anything wrong.

One night after a tiring day of work, Kevin went directly to the livery. He was so tired that he sneaked in through the back door, climbed into the hayloft, and fell asleep without eating his hunk of bread.

The next morning Kevin woke up to the voice of the liveryman. "What's this bread doing here? Hey, is somebody up there?"

Kevin realized instantly that somehow during the night, he had kicked the bread over the side of the loft onto the barn floor. He heard the man scurrying around.

"If you are a squatter up there, I'll pin you to the wall with this pitchfork!"

The ladder to the loft creaked as the man climbed up, and Kevin scrambled through the deep hay toward the other end of the barn. He had no idea how he was going to escape, but he had to get away. Maybe he could burrow into the hay and hide—but it was too late for that. The man was coming over the edge and had spotted him in the dim light.

Then Kevin saw a rope hanging from the roof. The bottom was tied to a nearby barn pole. He grabbed the rope and worked at the knot as the man with the pitchfork took giant steps through the hay in his direction. He saw what Kevin was trying to do and raised the pitchfork as though it were a spear he intended to throw.

Kevin got the rope free and jumped. As he swung out over the barn floor, he shimmied down the rope, hand over hand, until he landed safely near a horse stall. But the liveryman hadn't given up. He was running back to the ladder to cut off Kevin's exit.

Kevin ran through the door at top speed, with the liveryman not far behind.

So far Kevin had managed to stay away from policemen for over a week, but as he turned into the street—half looking behind him as he ran—he collided right into an officer.

" 'Scuse me, sir," he managed as he bounced off the stout officer and continued running.

"Grab that kid!" yelled the liveryman. "He's a vagrant. Been sleeping in my loft, and who knows what other mischief he's up to."

The shrill police whistle sounded in Kevin's ears as he ran for the waterfront.

He didn't know where he was going, but there was no time to plan. He just ran. Maybe the dock boss would give him a job mucking out the hold of a boat. He'd take anything, even if it meant working

on a boat . . . so long as it was tied up at the dock. All he cared about was not looking like a vagrant.

A morning mist smudged the harbor. On the dock

stood several men. Kevin recognized John Paton and Captain Fraser talking to three sailors. As Kevin sidled closer, he heard John Paton saying, "Yes, yes. We had very fine trip down the coast. I preached in many churches and was able to raise our full support. We already paid off Sam and Wilbur, and here's the money we owe you." He handed each sailor a handful of bills. "Now do you think you can crew for us when we head to the islands?"

The sailors stood there counting their money, shifting from one foot to the other.

While they considered John Paton's request, Kevin looked back in the direction he had come and saw the policeman rounding the corner. Fear propelled him toward the group of men. "Captain Fraser, here I am. I'm your boy. When do we sail?"

The captain frowned. "I thought this dock was as close as you wanted to get to the sea. What's the big change?"

But as he spoke, John Paton glanced toward the policeman. "I think the lad may have a little more incentive now than he had a couple weeks ago." He put his hand on Kevin's shoulder but turned again to the sailors. "The big question is whether you men will sign on with us in doing the Lord's work. What do you say?"

"We're all for doin' the Lord's work," one with a dark black beard said, "but what I need to know is whether we'll receive the Lord's honest pay. We got families to think about, you know."

"Well, that's settled, then," said John Paton. "Because the Lord has supplied us with an annual commitment to pay for the ship's expenses."

While they had been talking, Kevin noticed that the policeman had strolled closer. He leaned against the warehouse and kept an eye on Kevin.

Kevin rubbed his forehead with his hand. There didn't seem any way out of this one. It looked like either the sea or the sheep station . . . or maybe worse, depending on how angry the liveryman was.

The captain's words brought his attention back to the group. "And you, young man? We're going to be transporting missionary families from island to island, and we need a good cabin boy. You ready to sign?"

Kevin hesitated and looked over at the policeman still leaning against the warehouse. He swallowed hard, remembering the water closing over his head. "I . . . I can't swim," he gulped. His spirit sank. They'd never take him now. Looked like it was a sheep station for him.

John Paton nodded, but the captain's frown slowly turned into a wide grin. "You can't swim? Is that all? Well, son, half the men at sea can't swim."

"What?" Kevin looked dubiously at the sailors.

The captain was chuckling. "Look, lad, a couple hours from shore, even the best swimmer wouldn't have a chance. So we do our best to stay on board ship when we're at sea. Know what I mean?"

Kevin nodded slowly. "Guess it beats a sheep station." Maybe someday in some other port he could find a better job—a job on land.

Chapter 4

The Trader's Threat

With his knees feeling as weak as noodles, Kevin climbed into the longboat and rowed out to the *Dayspring* with Captain Fraser. What if he fell in?

But the longboat arrived safely, and after climbing aboard the *Dayspring*, the captain led him below deck and toward the bow. Pointing to one of the rope hammocks hanging from the beams he said, "You can have that one, and there's a sea chest to store your gear. Mr. Samson's the first mate. He'll be on board this evening. Do what he tells you." And then he left.

Kevin climbed into the hammock and turned over a couple times, trying various positions. That rope  webbing would feel as rough as a cargo net before morning. He didn't have any gear, but he got down and looked in the chest. There were some old clothes, a small New Testament, a prayer book, a few sheets of paper, and a pen and bottle of ink. It looked like someone else's gear. Kevin closed the lid. It didn't much matter. He didn't have any gear other than the clothes on his back and his packet of *Dayspring* shares—but he always kept them in the pouch around his neck.

About noon Mr. Samson came on board. He turned out to be the sailor with the dark beard Kevin had seen on the dock that morning. "Got the cabins clean?" the first mate asked.

"No, sir. The captain said you'd tell me what to do when you got here. I've just been—"

"Well, get busy then. We got three missionary families coming on board tomorrow, and everything needs to be shipshape."

He pointed to the same hammock the captain had given Kevin. "There's your berth, and that's your chest."

"But it's got someone else's gear in it." Kevin liked using the word *gear*. It sounded . . . "sea worthy."

"No matter," said Mr. Samson. "Keep it or toss it. It belonged to Robbie, but he won't be sailin' with us no more."

Kevin found a bucket and brushes and spent the rest of the day scrubbing the small cabins intended for the passengers. It was good having a real job. Sometimes he could feel a gentle motion or hear the creaking of the rigging as the *Dayspring* rode the small swells in the bay. It wasn't too bad. Maybe he could get used to being on the water after all.

The next afternoon, the captain's wife and little daughter came on board along with all the missionaries. They included Mr. and Mrs. Paton and their toddler, Mr. and Mrs. McNair, Mr. and Mrs. Niven, and Mrs. Ella and her small child.

He had only expected three families, so he had to work fast transferring the tins of biscuits that had been stored in the fourth cabin to the galley, and then he had to clean it, too. All the while, the other families kept asking him for help stowing their gear and getting extra blankets or candles or you-name-it. The list of errands never seemed to end.

Before Kevin got Mrs. Ella settled in her cabin, he heard Captain Fraser's clear voice giving orders to get the ship underway. Sailors ran back and forth on the deck above. The first feeling that the ship was moving made Kevin feel dizzy, and he reached out to grab something to steady himself. If he could just get up on deck, he thought, he could get his bearings and feel better, but he still had too much work to do.

Then it hit him: It was too late to turn back! He was headed for sea!

❖ ❖ ❖ ❖

The sun had set before Kevin got his break to go up on deck. He stood alone at the rail looking out at the orange and purples of the cloud-streaked sky.

Water hissed past the hull of the *Dayspring* accented by the soft slapping of small waves. Sometimes a sail would luff and snap in the wind. It was breathtaking.

"So,"—Kevin jumped at the sound of Rev. Paton's voice—"what do you think now that you've gotten yourself a job on a ship?"

Kevin looked at the bearded missionary and then out on the placid sea glittering in the sunset. "This isn't as bad as I had expected."

"Hmm. You haven't seen a storm yet, either." Paton chuckled. "But you'll do all right. Just trust in the Lord. By the way, why was that policeman eyeing you yesterday?"

It took some coaxing on Paton's part, but Kevin finally told the missionary how his mother had died, and without a place to live, he feared being sent to a sheep station.

"So you think working with sheep might be worse than going to sea? Is that what made you come running down to the docks?"

"I don't know. I just knew I didn't want to get caught."

The missionary leaned forward and put his elbows on the ship's rail and his chin in his hands as he stared out to sea. Finally he said, "You need more of a purpose to your life than just avoiding the wilderness. How old are you, anyway?"

"Almost fourteen."

"When I was two years younger than you, I went to work for a surveying company, but I already knew that God wanted me to become a missionary. So, each day during my lunch hour, I would go sit by myself and study my school lessons. My boss noticed this and thought I might be smart enough to learn surveying. He offered me a promotion and special training if I would agree to work for him for seven years.

" 'Thank you, sir,' I said. 'That is most kind. But I can't do it. I might agree for three or four years, but not seven. That would put me too far behind in my preparations.'

" 'Preparations for what, lad?' He sounded a little offended. 'Why would you refuse an offer that many gentlemen's sons would be proud of?'

" 'Because,' I said, 'I have already dedicated my life to another Master.'

"The supervisor frowned. 'And who would that be?'

" 'To the Lord Jesus,' I told him. 'I must prepare as swiftly as possible to serve Him as a missionary.'

" 'You fool!' the supervisor roared as he lunged at me. 'Accept my offer, or you are fired on the spot!'

"Well, I stood my ground and got fired for it, but God still provided. Now, Kevin, why do you think I did such a thing?"

Kevin squirmed a little and looked down at the foaming sea hissing past the ship. "I don't know. Sounds like it would have been a better job than working on a sheep station or going to sea."

"Without a doubt . . . and good money, too. But I had a goal, and that goal kept me on course until it brought me here where I am now serving the Lord as a missionary in the South Seas."

Rev. Paton was silent for a few minutes, then asked, "Have you received the Lord Jesus as your Savior, lad?"

Kevin smiled. "Oh yes, sir. My mama taught me the Bible."

"That's good. That's good. But the Bible says, 'Ye are not your own. For ye are bought with a price: therefore glorify God in your body, and in your spirit, which are God's.' Jesus saved you for a purpose, Kevin. And it's your job to find out what that purpose is. It will give direction to your life."

Kevin didn't know what to do with that little sermon. Pretty soon he felt Paton's hand on his shoulder. It patted him a couple times, and then the missionary walked on down the deck.

Kevin stared out on the darkening sea not knowing how he would discover God's purpose for his life. He and his mama had always been too busy just trying to survive.

✧ ✧ ✧ ✧

Three days later, Kevin was certain that life at sea couldn't be God's purpose for him. A storm had come up, causing the *Dayspring* to pitch like a bucking horse over the waves, and Kevin's stomach pitched right along with it. In fact, it "pitched" *up* everything he tried to eat. Several of the missionaries were also sick, but Kevin felt so weak and dizzy that he curled up in his hammock and closed his eyes.

Someone yanked on his hammock so hard that he tumbled out. "Captain wants to see you . . . on deck," said Mr. Samson.

Kevin got up off his hands and knees where he had fallen and followed the first mate up the ladder.

"Where've you been?" growled Captain Fraser.

"In my hammock."

"You're crew. On this ship you work—specifically, you serve those missionaries who are sick down below. Help 'em clean up. Bring 'em what they need. Now get goin'!"

"But, sir—" Kevin grabbed for the mast to keep his balance as the ship lurched. "I've been seasick, too."

"You've been what?" The captain waved his arm in disgust. "Mr. Samson, please tell this landlubber what it's like in the navy or on a merchant ship. Set him straight!" And then he walked away.

"You got it easy here, boy, and you ought to be grateful. Why, if you was in the navy, you'd be flogged for not lookin' lively when given an order."

"Yes, sir."

Kevin went below deck, hanging on to anything solid to keep his balance. He knocked on the cabin doors and offered his help. In a while, he realized that he was feeling better. He didn't know if it was the activity or getting his mind off his own troubles, but he didn't throw up anymore.

Fortunately, the wind subsided during the night,

and the next morning the seas were calm as the sun began burning through the fog.

About noon, one of the sailors yelled, "Land ho! Land ho!" And sure enough, as the mist cleared, the dim outline of an island could be seen to the northeast.

"It's New Caledonia," announced Captain Fraser as the passengers all came up on deck. "We can refill our water kegs there. The New Hebrides is just one day farther."

But they were not alone in the bay when they dropped anchor that evening. The captain lowered his looking glass. "It's the *Hopeful*."

"It might be registered as the *Hopeful*," muttered John Paton, "but that's the most unhopeful ship in the South Seas."

"Why is that, dear?" Mrs. Paton was standing by her husband, her hand through his arm.

"She's the sandalwood trading ship I caught a ride on from Tanna to Sydney three years ago when I had to escape. But they trade in a lot more than sandalwood." Paton raised his voice. "Captain, remember my telling you about Williams and McNeil from the *Hopeful*? I think we should anchor as far from them as possible."

"Consider it done," said the captain. "Ready to come about, Mr. Samson."

The first mate shouted the captain's orders to the crew as the ship turned into the wind and dropped anchor. Kevin stood near the Patons with his back to the ship's rail, watching the sailors up in the rigging.

Mrs. Paton persisted. "I still don't understand. What's wrong with the *Hopeful*?"

"Nothing's wrong with the ship. It's those who run it, a boatswain named Williams and an agent called McNeil. They're slave traders. They kidnap natives and take them to sugar plantations in Queensland, Australia." Paton shook his head. "I'm afraid I made a real enemy of Boatswain Williams over the slave issue. I told the authorities in Sydney."

"Do you think they'll bother us?"

"Margaret, they'll bother us any way they can. You can be sure of that. They're the ones who sent the three sailors with measles among the natives when I was on Tanna. The natives had no resistance to the disease, so nearly a third of the people on the island died. It was . . . it was calculated murder."

Mrs. Paton shuddered. "Why would they do a thing like that?"

"They knew that in their superstition, the natives would blame me. Williams and McNeil hoped that the natives would drive me off the island, which they finally did."

"But why?"

"Because Christians don't buy guns and rum, and so they don't like missionaries making Christians of the natives. But in God's name, I am now their enemy, too."

"John, don't say such a thing!"

"Well, call it what you will, but I'm committed to stopping their slave trading."

Kevin's eavesdropping was interrupted by a shout. The anchors were down, and the first mate called Kevin to help furl some of the sails.

✧ ✧ ✧

The sun was near setting, but John Paton and Mr. Niven, one of the other missionaries, wanted to go ashore and visit the native village that could be seen just beyond the beach.

"I'm not sure it's a good idea to go in this late," said the captain. "What if the natives aren't friendly?"

"They can't be too hostile. The *Hopeful*'s longboat has been on the beach since we anchored, and you can see some of their sailors going back and forth from it to the village. That's why we're eager to get ashore. We want to warn those poor people about the slave traders before they get tricked into going on board the *Hopeful*," said Mr. Paton.

When the *Dayspring*'s boat was put in the water, Mr. Samson ordered Kevin to go along, too, and help fill a couple water kegs while the missionaries talked to the villagers.

Kevin could see a fire burning on the beach as the *Dayspring*'s boat shot through the surf and scraped to a halt on the coral sand. Standing in the fire's light were a couple white men and several native people.

"Well, if it isn't that meddling missionary," sneered one of the white men.

"McNeil, Williams," acknowledged Rev. Paton calmly. "I can't say that I'm happy to still see you in these waters."

"We were here before you, and we'll be here long after we drive you away again."

"What's that mean?"

"I heard why you've got that ship, the *Dayspring*. But it won't do you any good." The man named McNeil jabbed a finger at Paton. "I'm warning you. You escaped from Tanna once, but you won't do it again! I'll see the *Dayspring* on the bottom of the sea and you with it before I'll allow any more missionaries to disrupt our business."

Chapter 5

Feasting With Cannibals

The *Hopeful* was still anchored in the harbor when Rev. Paton reluctantly gave Captain Fraser the okay to leave New Caledonia the next morning. It took a full twenty-four hours to sail to the island of Anatom in the New Hebrides. Captain Fraser traced their route on the ship's map to the southernmost island in the group for the curious missionaries. And Kevin listened intently as Rev. Paton told the story of how, over fifteen years earlier, John Geddie and John Inglis and their wives had established such a successful mission on the island that some thirty-five hundred people became Christians. Many of them had accompanied other missionaries to other islands

to help spread the Gospel. "Some went with me to Tanna," Paton said soberly, "and were killed for their faith. I barely escaped with my own life."

Now Anatom acted as the mission headquarters for the area. After anchoring in the harbor and going ashore, the Patons and the other newly arriving missionaries had a happy reunion with the older missionaries who had gathered to welcome them and to have their annual planning meeting.

After scrubbing the deck and doing other maintenance chores on the *Dayspring*, all the sailors were free to go ashore. They were encouraged to join the worship services that the missionaries held daily.

Kevin was surprised to hear John Paton ask to return to the island of Tanna, which had driven him out three years earlier. Apparently the other missionaries were surprised at his request, as well. "What has changed?" asked one of the men. "Those tribes are still fighting each other, and if you get in the middle, they'd turn on you again, too."

Before John Paton could answer, another missionary chimed in. "And word gets around, too. If there was more violence against missionaries on Tanna, and our people heard about it, it might encourage them to attack us. We can't take a chance on any more attacks on Tanna. Why don't you go to Aniwa Island?"

John Paton stood up. "I want to return to Tanna because my work there is not finished. Besides . . ." He looked toward his wife as though seeking her reassurance. Then he said, "My first wife and our little boy are buried there."

"I still think we ought to concentrate on some of the more peaceful islands," said the first missionary. "The more people accept Christ and cease their violence, the easier it will be to tackle the tougher islands later."

Paton raised his hands, palms upward. "But I believe there is hope for Tanna. Don't forget that old Chief Nowar was coming around. God was softening his heart. Sometimes he protected me."

"But you also said he abandoned you in your most desperate hour. I don't think he can be trusted. Besides, he is chief of only one of the tribes on the island, and not the most powerful tribe, either."

Kevin's head was turning from side to side as he listened to first one person speak and then another, learning more and more what it had been like when John Paton was on Tanna.

"It's true that Nowar was not very reliable, but on the other hand, I gave him plenty of opportunities, and he didn't eat me! Now, that's got to count for something."

Everyone laughed.

"Seriously," continued Paton, "think of the witness to the other islands if the Gospel took root on Tanna and brought peace among those warring people! I know God can do it. I know He wants to, and I'd like another chance to be part of the effort."

But the other missionaries continued to disapprove. Too many lives had been lost the first time on that violent island. They decided it would be better to establish a foothold on the small nearby island of Aniwa. It had fewer tribes and less violence.

Reluctantly, Paton conceded. "Well, if I can't locate on Tanna, then I want to visit there. Certainly we would be safe enough with the *Dayspring* waiting offshore."

Some of the other missionaries nodded, some shrugged, and so it was decided that the *Dayspring* would deliver all the other missionaries to their islands—the old ones to their home islands and the new ones to their new mission stations—and then it would come back to Tanna while John Paton made a visit. After that it would sail over to Aniwa, where the Patons would begin their new work.

In the two weeks that followed, Kevin began to think that he might learn to love—or at least tolerate—the sea. The weather was calm, and each island was a new adventure. Living in Sydney his whole life, he had never imagined such beauty! Most of the islands had been formed from volcanoes, five of which were still active. Coral reefs partially surrounded many of the islands, making the approach by ship challenging. But the beautiful beaches backed by rich green forest and dramatic mountains were worth the effort.

At every island, canoes of natives paddled out to meet the *Dayspring*. The natives from the islands where the older missionaries lived marveled at the new ship. They understood that no longer would the "missi," as they called the missionary, have to wait for a trading ship to receive supplies or take a trip

down to Anatom.

In good weather, the native people sometimes traveled between the islands in their large seagoing canoes, and so the news of the new "missi ship," the *Dayspring*, preceded its arrival at several islands.

On the islands, Kevin was amazed to discover how excited many of the natives were at the arrival of the new missionaries. After some long conversations where translation was difficult, Paton finally announced to those on board the ship, "I finally discovered why they want a missionary of their own. They all have heard reports of how the cannibals on Tanna killed the missionary helpers from Anatom and drove me off the island. They thought that would be the end of all missionaries in these islands. But even though we were driven off, now I and several new missionaries have come back. They count that as great courage.

"One said, 'We killed and drove away the missionaries. We broke down your houses and robbed you. If that had happened to us, we would never return. But you came back in a beautiful new ship with more and more missionaries. And is it to make money like the traders? No! No! You are here only to do us good and tell us about Jesus. If your God makes you do all that, we may worship Him, too.'"

Mrs. Paton clapped her hands. "Praise God! He has turned a terrible event into something good."

That evening the sky turned gray and the wind kicked the waves into whitecaps before the *Dayspring* dropped anchor in Port Resolution on the island of Tanna. As at the other islands, several canoes came out to greet the ship. Rev. Paton called to many of the natives in their own language. He pointed out various ones, announcing their names, but the waves were too high to allow the frail canoes to get too close to the *Dayspring*.

Later, when everyone sat down to dinner, John Paton had a worried expression. "I didn't see Chief Nowar this afternoon. I hope he is well. I can't imagine why he didn't come out to greet us. Maybe tomorrow we can go ashore and find him."

That night the rocking of the ship in the wind unsettled Kevin, and he went up on deck. The clouds were breaking up, and the moon shone through. Across the bay, Kevin could see a dark shape on the water. It seemed to be moving. Yes, yes . . . it *was* moving. The faint clang of a bell and the muffled voice of someone giving orders reached his ears.

Kevin strained his eyes until he couldn't tell what he was seeing. Then he closed them for a moment and looked again. The dark shape was still there, though it no longer seemed to move.

Another ship had anchored in Port Resolution Bay.

✧ ✧ ✧

In the morning, the other ship was still there. Captain Fraser was studying it with his telescope when Kevin came up on deck.

"It's the *Hopeful* again," he muttered. "And they've already sent a boat to shore. Boy, go down and tell Rev. Paton what's happening. Tell him that if he wants to talk to his natives before McNeil and

Williams get to them, he'd better get up here quick."

Then he shouted toward the back of the ship. "Mr. Samson, prepare to launch the longboat."

"Aye, aye, Captain."

Kevin came back up on deck with Rev. Paton a few minutes later helping him carry an armload of gifts for Chief Nowar—a bag of fishhooks, several axes and machetes, and some flint and steel for lighting fires.

"Kevin, bring those with us in the longboat. I want to assure Nowar of my goodwill from the very beginning. He might have stayed away yesterday thinking I am angry with him. But I'm not, and I want to demonstrate that to him."

Kevin's eyebrows went up. He was going ashore? His heart beat with both fear and excitement. He hurried to join the shore expedition of Rev. Paton, the captain, and three sailors. Kevin took his seat at one of the oars and did his best to stay in rhythm as they rowed toward shore.

The bay was well sheltered, but the choppy waves kicked up by the night's wind sent high surf crashing onto the beach. Kevin bit his lip and pulled hard on his oar, taking brief glances over his shoulder at the waves they would have to row through. What if the boat turned sideways? What if it flipped? What if he got thrown into the water? All the old fears came back, but he kept rowing.

Finally, about a hundred yards from shore, the captain, who was sitting in the stern handling the tiller, said, "Steady . . ." Kevin and the other sailors stopped rowing as the longboat rocked up and down over the swells rolling beneath it toward shore. "Steady, mates. We don't need a bath today. . . . Now! *Pull* for all you're worth, lads."

Kevin pulled, all right. He pulled as though his life depended upon it.

In an instant the longboat seemed to rise up into the air as though the nose of a whale were under it. It shot forward toward the shore, and Kevin had to fight the urge to drop the oar and grab onto the gunwale. But he kept rowing in time with the other sailors.

Spray and foam rose all around them, and then *crunch*, they hit the beach and the boat came to a stop so fast that Kevin fell over backwards. He got out into knee-deep water and helped drag the boat a little farther up onto the beach.

Suddenly his knees seemed so weak that he sat down in the white sand. Embarrassed, he said, "Now, this is nice and warm." But no one seemed to pay any attention. Rev. Paton was talking to the natives who had gathered around.

"They say Chief Nowar is at his village talking to some other white men," Paton translated. "Let's go."

Kevin shouldered the sea bag with the missionary's gifts and followed Paton and the captain and several of the natives as they crossed the sand and walked through a field of tall grass toward the jungle. The three sailors stayed with the boat as the other natives tried to trade things they had made for the sailors' shirts and buttons and hats. Used to such attention, the sailors laughed and waved them off.

The missionary, the captain, and Kevin followed the trail through the jungle for a mile, winding around the base of Mount Yasur, the active volcano he had seen from the bay. They had turned a corner and started down a small hill when they heard voices ahead. As they got closer, they recognized English, and then from the dense growth emerged Agent McNeil and Mr. Williams.

"Well, who have we here?" McNeil crossed his arms and tilted his head back. "You still trying to convert old Nowar? It'll never happen. He loves his rum too much." McNeil and Williams laughed and stepped aside, bowing in mockery as Paton and his party passed.

"It's not *his* rum," said Paton through clenched teeth when he got even with McNeil and faced him eye to eye. "It's *your* rum. You corrupt the natives with it."

"Well, business is business," McNeil said with a shrug and went on up the trail.

Another five minutes brought Paton and those with him to a village. In front of one of the huts an old man struggled to his feet, leaning heavily on an ornately carved staff. "See that band of white shells around his arm?" said John Paton. "That shows he's a chief. That's Nowar. He's not the most powerful chief on this island, but he's the only one who ever befriended me . . . though sometimes he lost his courage."

The chief's woolly hair and beard were as white and wild as sea-foam, but his eyes were bright and his toothless smile as broad as his face when he reached out toward John Paton. "Missi, my Missi, you have come back!" He grasped Paton's extended hand while the missionary translated the chief's words.

The chief kept patting Paton's arm, looking up from his crippled stance to study the missionary's face as though he couldn't believe what he saw.

"Come, come. We will eat together. Those terrible traders said you were coming, so I prepared a great feast for you." He turned and, holding on to Paton with one hand, he pulled him toward his hut. Then he turned back with a gleam in his eye and wagged his finger toward the missionary. "And just for you, I have roasted only goats and yams—no humans for your feast." Paton laughed as he translated.

They sat on mats in a circle before the chief's hut as Paton delivered the gifts Kevin had carried. Soon other tribal members began bringing food for them to eat.

"You weren't listening to those traders, were you?" Paton asked the old chief.

"Oh no, Missi. Why would I listen to those lying thieves? They bring only trouble. I just kicked them out of my village. Maybe you passed them on your way here. But you don't need to worry. Now that you are here, I will listen only to you. We will help you build a fine new home and then—"

Paton raised his hand. "But I can't stay. We're here only for a visit. I just wanted to see how you were doing, old friend."

"Oh, but you must stay," said the chief. "Things will be different now. There will be no more war. I will protect you. Look at this great feast I have prepared for you."

But Kevin noticed that the meat brought to him already had large slices cut off of it, and among the delicious yams were the empty skins of ones already eaten. It looked more like the leftovers of a feast celebrated with someone else. Possibly the traders?

Some time later, Kevin felt the urge to relieve himself. He got up and headed toward the bushes at the edge of the jungle. But as he walked around the chief's hut, he glanced in and noticed a pile of guns and three kegs of rum.

Chapter 6

Guns and Kegs

Chief Nowar carried on so excitedly about Paton returning to Tanna that Captain Fraser finally spoke up. "Tell the old chief that I will *not* return you to Tanna. Tell him that the missionary council on Anatom told me not to unload his luggage and supply boxes on the shore of your island."

Paton had not finished translating the captain's comments before the chief interrupted, and Paton had to translate for him. "Don't land them, then. I would not want you to disobey the council. All you need to do is throw them overboard, and my men will catch them in their canoes and bring them safely to shore." He raised his finger and closed his eyes.

"Not one box will get wet."

"No, no, no. You don't understand. I'm not going to do anything to move the Patons onto Tanna."

"Fine," said the chief. "Just point his luggage out to us and you will have no further trouble. We will manage everything for Missi."

"The Patons are going to Aniwa!"

"Wait! Did you say *the Patons*? Oh, Missi, do you have a new wife?"

"Yes, and a little son."

The chief began clapping his hands. "I am so glad. I must meet them."

"We will come ashore tomorrow. I want to show her where I lived. You can meet her then."

✧ ✧ ✧ ✧

The next day when the longboat set off from the *Dayspring* to ferry the Patons to shore, Kevin went along again, this time to help carry Little Bob, the Patons' toddler. The waves were much smaller. Kevin pulled on his oar and watched over his shoulder, but the beach landing was much easier.

The chief and several of the villagers were there to greet them. With great flourish, Chief Nowar introduced a tall, handsome native whom Kevin had not seen the day before. John Paton became very interested, greeting the man with much ceremony.

"This is a visiting chief from Aniwa, the island on which we will be settling," Paton explained to the landing party. "His name is Pavingin." He looked at the man to see if he had pronounced his name correctly. The tall chief smiled and nodded his approval.

Then Chief Nowar stepped forward and urgently said something that Paton translated. " 'Here, here,' he says. 'This is for Missi's wife.' "

The old chief busily directed two women how to hold a large banana leaf umbrella over Mrs. Paton to shade her from the bright sun.

When they got started, the nearly naked natives and fully dressed Europeans made a contrasting procession inland. With Little Bob riding piggyback, Kevin fell into line behind Mrs. Paton.

"We *must* teach them to wear clothing," she said to her husband.

"Yes, my dear," he said dryly, "just as soon as we convince them to stop eating their enemies."

The tall chief, Pavingin, fell into line at the end of the procession.

When they were only a short way into the grassy field, Rev. Paton turned off the trail and began searching around in the tall reeds and grass. "Here, here," he said as he tripped over an old log and came upon the ruins of a crumbling fireplace. "This was our first home."

Everyone stood around quietly as the missionary looked around . . . at the higher ground with its dense jungle, Mount Yasur in the distance with a small steam cloud waving slowly like a flag from the top, and then back at the sea.

"It was a mistake to try to live here. It's nearly a swamp. Too many mosquitoes. Too much disease."

He was quiet for several minutes. Then he led the others a little farther through the tall grass and came to a memorial built of coral stones. He closed his eyes and tilted his head up. "Mary Ann and I landed on November 5, 1858. She gave birth to our baby, Peter, just three months later, and then she died on March third." He took a deep breath and wiped his forehead. "Peter died a couple weeks later—March twentieth. There was nothing I could do."

The new Mrs. Paton moved closer to her husband and slipped her arm around his waist.

"Many times I came down here to pray, and God gave me strength to carry on."

After a long silence, Paton said, "Finally I figured out that I had to move to someplace that would be more healthy—higher ground, refreshed by the cool trade winds." He turned and headed back to the trail, and everyone followed.

Kevin noticed that the visiting chief often kept somewhat apart from the other natives, and Chief Nowar never gave him any orders. *Pavingin must be an important man,* Kevin thought.

The small party climbed to a nearby hilltop. On it was the ruins of a house still partially standing. Little Bob was fussing, so Kevin handed him to his mother and rolled his aching shoulders. It amazed him how mothers could hold their children for long periods without wearing themselves out.

"I finally moved up here." Paton looked through the doorway. The door itself had been broken down long ago. He pounded his fist on the doorjamb. "Still pretty solid. I used some of the wood from our old house and many planks from an old shipwreck. It was much better here."

Chief Nowar went into a long speech, gesturing at the surrounding countryside and the ruins and then at himself. Finally Paton translated. "He says that he and his people will help me rebuild this house bigger and better than before if only I will return to Tanna. I hardly have the heart to keep telling him no."

Half an hour later, Kevin hoisted Little Bob onto his back as the group headed down the hill toward Nowar's village. The chief stopped under a large chestnut tree and began pointing up into the branches and talking excitedly again.

"He's saying," said Paton, "that this is the tree where I hid when the warring tribes were going back and forth trying to kill each other. I was so scared, I probably couldn't have found it."

"How long did you stay up there?" asked Kevin.

"Oh, most of a day, I guess." He nodded toward the chief. "Nowar had been sheltering me from a large crowd of armed warriors. I had prayed when they were at the foot of the hill leading up to his village, and suddenly they stopped and became silent. Then the warriors turned around and began to march back the way they had come.

"Nowar and his people cried out in great excitement, 'Jehovah has heard Missi's prayer and is protecting us.' But the pressure got to him. The enemy chiefs threatened to kill him and all his people, so he

brought me here and told me to hide up in this tree.

"About midnight, Nowar's son came and got me and led me to the shore, where I escaped in a canoe."

The old chief was able to follow enough of Paton's story that he jumped in again, urging Paton to translate for him to the others.

"See, you were safe even though I let you down, but now I will protect you. Why don't you stay?"

"No, no. I cannot." Paton shook his head and turned to his wife.

Thinking that the missionary's gesture meant that Margaret Paton didn't want to live on Tanna, Nowar turned to her and actually got down on his crippled knees and began begging her.

"What is he saying? What does he want?" she asked.

Paton laughed. "He thinks you are afraid of not having enough food on Tanna. He says, 'Plenty food. Plenty food.' As long as he has bananas and yams, you will eat and grow fat."

Margaret Paton turned away with a big sigh. "That's not it. Tell him that's not it! For heaven's sake, when will he stop this begging?"

Kevin also wondered when Nowar would accept the Patons' decision not to locate on Tanna. But more importantly he began to wonder *why* it mattered so much to the old chief. What were his motives?

All the way back to the beach, Kevin tried to figure it out. Something didn't seem right. He thought about the feast with Nowar the day before. The chief had made it seem like it was all in honor of his Missi, but Kevin thought that maybe the feast had first been served to Agent McNeil and Williams.

There were also the guns and rum kegs that Kevin had seen. The guns had been lying in a pile. Anyone's personal guns would have been in a rack or sitting up somewhere. These had looked like the traders had brought them—possibly in payment for . . . for what? Kevin hadn't seen any evidence that Nowar and his people had been logging sandalwood for trade. So what had Nowar given in exchange for the guns and rum?

By the time they had reached the beach, Kevin decided that Nowar's eagerness to get the Patons to stay on the island must indeed have something to do with the traders. Maybe he had promised the traders he would get rid of the missionaries. Wasn't that what the traders had said they wanted? What they had threatened?

At the beach, Kevin was ready to return to the *Dayspring* with the Patons and the captain, but Mr. Samson had come ashore in a native canoe and was waiting with the sailors near the longboat.

"Kevin, I want you to stay ashore with me," the first mate said. "We need to cut a new spar from one of those trees up on that hill. I'll need your help."

After carrying Little Bob all afternoon, Kevin wasn't eager for another assignment, especially one that might involve cutting down a tree, trimming the branches, and dragging it down to the beach. But he wasn't on this island for a vacation.

It was dark when they got back with the newly cut spar. Chief Nowar and the other native had not returned to their village but had set up camp on the beach with a large fire and some lean-to huts made of banana leaves. Rather than join them, Mr. Samson and Kevin built a fire of their own a quarter of a mile down the beach. The first mate also served as the ship's carpenter, and he set to work peeling the bark off the thin tree trunk and shaping it into a spar for the *Dayspring*.

"Why don't you run down there and see if you can get us something to eat?" he said to Kevin.

"In the dark?"

"Why not? You can't possibly get lost. Don't go in the jungle. Don't go in the water. Just keep walking down the beach toward that other fire."

"Yeah, but those people are cannibals."

"They're not going to do anything in plain view of the *Dayspring*."

Reluctantly, Kevin headed down the beach into the dark with the waves gently breaking on his right and the night sounds of the jungle on the left. The farther he went from Mr. Samson's fire, and the closer he got to Chief Nowar's fire, the slower he walked.

A deep rumble came from inland somewhere, and then the earth gave a shake like a ship bumping too hard into a dock. Kevin braced himself and looked up at the top of the volcano. A red glow pulsed against the smoke that belched from its bald peak.

Chapter 7

Rough Surf

The earth shook again, and this time Kevin dropped to his hands and knees. But the waves kept breaking on the shore, and the night birds kept calling from the jungle as if nothing unusual were happening. Kevin looked back at Mr. Samson and down the beach to the villagers.

When no one else seemed concerned about the volcano, Kevin finally got up and walked on toward the villagers' fire. But he kept an eye on the top of Mount Yasur, trying to think what he would do if it blew. . . . He had no idea! Run into the sea, maybe?

Shaded from their firelight by one of the temporary huts, Kevin approached the camp unseen. Some of the villagers were working on another shelter of banana leaves, but the two chiefs were sitting by the fire talking earnestly. Kevin was about to step out from behind the shelter when he heard Chief Nowar say something about "Missi Paton."

He stayed in the shadows and watched. With a scornful frown on his face, Pavingin waved his hands away, dismissing whatever Nowar had said. Then Pavingin began speaking very earnestly, shaking his finger at Nowar. Suddenly he held up his arms like he was holding a rifle and said, *"Bang! Bang!"* Then he pantomimed drinking something. He made big circles with his arms toward himself as though he were loading himself with more and more. During his speech, Kevin suddenly heard Pavingin saying, "McNeil promise. McNeil promise. McNeil promise."

Kevin caught his breath. The visiting chief was talking about guns and rum and Agent McNeil only a few moments after Nowar had been speaking of John Paton. Had the sandalwood trader promised them guns and rum to kill the missionary? It was the only explanation that seemed to fit.

Then Nowar became very upset, but Kevin couldn't determine why. Did he want to protect Paton as he had claimed that afternoon, or was he jealous that Pavingin might collect the rewards of guns and rum before he did?

Finally the old chief cut the string of white shells from his arm and tied them around Pavingin's arm. Nowar was so animated and upset that Kevin couldn't recognize any of his words except "Missi

Paton." It was "Missi Paton this" and "Missi Paton that," yelled with great passion. And then Chief Nowar raised his heavy walking staff above Pavingin's head like a club. With obvious fear, the visiting chief kept nodding his head and holding his hands up as though to protect himself or plead for mercy . . . or was he promising to carry out Nowar's plan?

Kevin couldn't be sure.

Slowly, Kevin backed away and headed down the beach toward Mr. Samson. His steps quickened involuntarily. He tried to slow down and keep calm, but he began imagining the villagers chasing him with spears and clubs, and suddenly he broke into a run. Faster and faster. He had never run so fast in his life.

He arrived at the first mate's fire just as the longboat skidded onto the beach.

"Captain's a little concerned about the volcano," said one of the sailors. "He wants you to get back to the ship as soon as possible."

Mr. Samson looked around and saw Kevin standing there trying to catch his breath. "Good, you're back," he said to Kevin. "Tie that rope onto our new spar, and then roll it into the water. Let's get out of here!"

✧ ✧ ✧ ✧

They arrived at the *Dayspring* amid preparations for immediate departure, but the captain said, "I want to be ready, but we won't lift anchor before morning unless Mount Yasur blows. I wouldn't want to run into that coral reef that hooks around the point while we are trying to get out of Port Resolution."

There were no more rumbles from the volcano during the night, but before they departed the next morning, three canoes came alongside the *Dayspring*. They held Chief Nowar, Chief Pavingin, and several village men. Rev. Paton went to the ship's railing to say good-bye.

After they had talked a few minutes, Paton turned around and called, "Captain Fraser, this visitor from Aniwa, Chief Pavingin, would like to return with us to his island. He wants to know if we can tie a line to his canoe and tow him back."

"I wouldn't recommend it," said the captain. "It looks like a calm day, but you can never tell when a rogue wave might capsize a canoe like that, especially if we were pulling it. Just have him come on board. Then it won't matter much if the canoe rolls over."

Kevin wanted to tell John Paton right then about the conversation he had overheard the night before on the beach, but there was no time. Mr. Samson was giving orders to raise the anchor, set the sails, and get the ship underway. As the weeks had gone by, Kevin had learned various duties of a regular sailor, but now those tasks left him no time to talk to John Paton about the tall native chief that had just climbed over the railing to become a passenger on the *Dayspring* as it sailed to Aniwa.

They had been to sea a little over an hour when Mr. Samson said, "Kevin, start bringing all the Patons' gear up on deck. We're almost there."

"Almost where?"

"Aniwa. Are you trying to be smart? I thought you'd outgrown questioning my orders."

"No, sir." Kevin jumped up from the coil of rope on which he had been relaxing. "I just didn't see any land. . . . Is that it?" He gazed ahead at a small, low-lying island covered with green.

"Yes, that's it! Not much to see, is it?"

"No, sir. Do people live there?"

"So they say. Now you better start bringing their gear and supplies up on deck."

Kevin went below, shaking his head. There was no smoking volcano, no jagged peaks. Even the trees—if that's what they were—looked too small to provide much protection from the hurricanes that periodically swept the South Pacific.

As he was getting the Patons' belongings, he heard the first mate give orders to drop the anchor. How could they have gotten into harbor so quickly? But when Kevin came up on deck dragging some of the bags the Patons would be taking ashore, he saw that they had not anchored within a pleasant harbor.

He pointed at a line of pounding surf a hundred feet from the ship that separated it from the island a hundred yards beyond. "Is that a reef?" he asked a nearby sailor.

"Sure is, and it circles the island like a belt."

"Then how can we get to shore?"

"Straight through. There's supposed to be a little gap up there somewhere."

Kevin shuddered as he looked at the pounding waves. This was nothing like riding the waves into the beach back at Tanna. What would happen if the boat got caught in a current and smashed into the reef? It would become a tumbling bundle of sticks in a matter of minutes.

The old terror of drowning gripped him, and he swayed back and forth.

"What's the matter with you, boy?" said Mr. Samson. "You've got a lot of supplies to bring up here. Get a move on. We've got five or six trips to shore. I don't want to be doing this in the dark."

Kevin stumbled down the stairs. What were the chances he could remain on board ship? Would the captain insist he go ashore? Maybe he could say something.

"You don't look too good. Are you feeling all right, Kevin?" asked Mrs. Paton. "Here, would you hold Bob a moment? I forgot something in our cabin."

When she came back, he handed the little boy back to her and hurried past so she wouldn't ask any more questions. He was breathing like he had run a mile, and he began to feel lightheaded. He couldn't go through those waves. He'd be dumped and drowned for sure. He had to think of something.

When he finished carrying the Patons' personal luggage up to the deck, he headed back down to begin bringing up the supplies they would need on the island, but Mr. Samson called to him. "Get over to the starboard side and help launch that longboat. I want you to help take the first load in. Some of the bigger men will bring up those barrels and crates."

Kevin continued down the steps as though he hadn't heard Mr. Samson.

"Kevin Gilmore," boomed Mr. Samson's voice, "get back up on deck and help launch that longboat. What's the matter with you today? Has your hearing gone bad?"

"Aye, aye, sir," said Kevin. He staggered across the deck as though the ship were rolling in a bad storm. He could now hear the thundering roar of the waves breaking across the coral reef, but he avoided looking at the scary sea.

Once the longboat was launched, and the Patons were seated in it with some of their belongings, Kevin took his place at an oar, careful to keep his back to the waves crashing across the reef. They pulled away from the *Dayspring* with Captain Fraser standing in the stern of the boat, moving the rudder with his knees and shading his eyes with his hand so he could see the blue water through the reef.

"Steady as she goes, now, boys. . . . All right, I can see it now. Hold up on the port. No! No! No! Kevin, I said hold up on the port. You forget what side you're sitting on?"

A moment later the captain said, "All ahead, now. Easy. This is mighty narrow."

As Kevin pulled on his oar, he kept his eyes focused on the floorboards and the stagnant water

that sloshed back
and forth under them in the bot-
tom of the boat. He could feel the swells lifting and
dropping the small boat as it eased forward through
the channel.

The chubby legs of Little Bob appeared in his
vision. Kevin looked up. The toddler was leaning
over the gunwale not far from him while his mother
in her seat near the back of the boat was busy
digging for something in one of their bags. The boat

bucked more violently as they neared the breakers, and suddenly Little Bob's feet came off the floor. The child lost his balance and began to fall over the side.

Kevin leaped from his seat, flipping his oar into the air, and dove for the child. His shoulder crashed headlong into the gunwale as he grabbed Bob and tipped him back into the boat. But in an instant the boat dropped into a valley and Kevin lost his own balance and fell over the side into the churning waves.

Unlike the dark water he'd been pushed into from the dock in Sydney, this was brilliant white and blue. The current rolled him over until a huge, dark shape moved above him. It pushed him down, down— at least it seemed like down. From the corner of his eye he could see the jagged coral. The boat above was pushing him into the coral.

Crunch! The boat had pinned him against the reef.

The pain in his leg was so intense that he screamed out, sucking a lungful of stinging seawater the next instant.

Then suddenly he was on the surface, and strong hands were pulling him into the longboat. He coughed and choked as he lay on his stomach over a seat while one of the sailors slapped him hard on his back, forcing the water from his lungs. He vomited up what was left of his breakfast biscuit, leaving his throat and lungs burning.

Captain Fraser told one of the men to get the oar Kevin had dropped. Then he said, "That was a brave move, son. You saved the child. Are you all right?"

Kevin turned his head and looked back bleary-eyed at Mrs. Paton, who clutched Little Bob in her arms.

"I . . . I think I—*OW!*" he screamed as he moved his leg. "My leg!"

With the help of the sailor in the seat next to him, Kevin managed to turn over and sit on the bench seat while he leaned over to look at his leg. His pants from the knee down on his left leg were torn to shreds, and it was obvious that the dark stain was not water but blood.

John Paton quickly moved forward to kneel in front of Kevin. "I had medical training before I came out to the islands," he said. "Let me have a look."

Slowly, he peeled up Kevin's pant leg while the boy shivered from shock. A deep gash revealed ghastly white bone beneath. He gently moved Kevin's ankle from side to side. Kevin bit his lip as excruciating pain stabbed up and down his leg.

The missionary looked back over his shoulder. "I'm afraid, Captain, that he won't be much use to you for a while. It's definitely broken."

Chapter 8

"Rain" From Below

Glare from the white coral sand on the beach of Aniwa was giving Kevin a headache, but he welcomed its distraction from the pain in his leg. Rev. Paton had set the broken bone and splinted his leg between two barrel staves.

"You're going to have to keep off of that leg for a while," he said as he stood up and wiped the sweat off his face with a handkerchief.

"Can't I use crutches?"

"In time, but you'd best keep it elevated as much  as possible to keep down the swelling. I'm actually more worried about infection in that wound from the coral. I'll speak to the captain." Rev. Paton turned and headed

82

down to the water to meet the longboat, which was making its third trip to bring supplies in from the ship. Barrels and boxes and crates were stacked around Kevin in the shade of the palm trees. Nearby, Mrs. Paton watched over a sleeping Little Bob.

Natives from the island had gathered a short distance away where Chief Pavingin was lecturing them about the arriving missionaries. Kevin watched the group closely. Were they planning an attack once the *Dayspring* sailed away? Or was he telling the people that they should be happy to have their own "Missi"? He had to tell Rev. Paton about the inter-action he had witnessed the night before between Chief Nowar and Chief Pavingin.

The *Dayspring* remained anchored offshore for two days while John Paton and the captain scouted with some of the natives for a place where the mis-sionaries could build a house. "It's got to be on a piece of land that I can buy from the natives," Paton explained over dinner around the makeshift table on the beach. "I learned my lesson on Tanna. I can't allow any dispute over whether I can live there or not."

With mention of the danger from angry islanders, Kevin finally blurted out the conversation he had overheard.

Paton listened soberly. "Well, it's clear that McNeil and Williams continue doing their best to get rid of us." Then he punched his fist upward into the air. "But that's reason to feel encouraged. He knows God's Word makes a difference. It changes people.

People don't live the same old way. Even those who remain unbelievers are restrained from some of their evil in societies where the Gospel has taken root. It is the restraining power of the Holy Ghost. Thank God!"

"But . . . but aren't you going to confront Pavingin about it?" said Kevin. "He may be planning to kill you." He looked around. "Or all of us."

"He might be planning something." John Paton wiped his mouth with his napkin and brushed his beard. "But then probably so are half the people on this island."

When he noticed that everyone was staring at him, he added, "That doesn't mean they are going to succeed. We just have to be watchful. These islanders are an interesting people. If you are watching them, they won't attack you. It's when you get careless that they think they have a chance of getting away with it."

✧ ✧ ✧ ✧

The next morning, Captain Fraser said the *Dayspring* was set to sail. "Kevin, I want you to get yourself ready to come on out to the ship."

Kevin's stomach felt like a wet rag being wrung dry. He had managed to stay ashore since the accident. He could get around a little on some makeshift crutches, but the idea of going back on the water . . .

"Uh, Captain," said Rev. Paton, "it might be better to leave the boy here with us for a while longer.

That wound is still subject to infection, and I'm not sure how much good he would be to you on a rolling deck."

The captain lifted his hat and wiped his forehead. "That's true, but it could be a couple months before we get back this way."

"By then that leg should be mended," said Paton. "What do you say, Kevin? You willing to stick it out here with the sand and coconut trees and help us keep an eye on Chief Pavingin?"

Relief made Kevin feel weak. "Yes, sir. And as soon as my leg heals, I'll help you build your house, too."

❖ ❖ ❖ ❖

A week later Kevin was getting around quite well on his crutches, and the wound in his leg seemed to be free from infection. Rev. Paton led Kevin and Mrs. Paton, who carried Little Bob, to the top of a pleasant-looking mound that was above the malaria-ridden swamps along some of the shore.

"The natives are willing to sell this piece of land to us for our house for a few axes," he said. He began walking across it. "We can have everything from that banana tree down there to that bare patch of ground and then all the way down to the trail. What do you think?"

"It looks wonderful to me," said Mrs. Paton. She put Little Bob down and let him hold her finger as he toddled around.

"Good. Kevin, do you think that tomorrow you can help me begin construction?"

Kevin smiled and shrugged. "I'll do my best."

The first job the next morning was to level the ground. Kevin found he could lean on his crutches and work with a hoe breaking up the soil just about as fast as Rev. Paton could haul it off the peak of the mound.

After a while, he thought his hoe was hitting stones, but was startled to discover they were bones. After he had unearthed a few, Rev. Paton had a closer look. "Those are human bones." He dug around a little more. "There are hundreds of them here, just below the surface." Paton turned to one of the natives who stood watching nearby. "Is this a graveyard?"

When the native shrugged his shoulders, Paton ordered him to go find Chief Pavingin. When the chief finally arrived, Paton said, "Why are these bones here? Is this a graveyard for the tribe?"

"Oh no, Missi. It's not a graveyard for our people. It's just a rubbish heap."

"A rubbish heap of human bones? How did they get here?"

"We just dropped them when we finished."

"Finished? Finished? You mean you just threw these bones away when you had finished eating other people?"

"Of course, Missi. You don't think we eat *bones*, do you?" He shook his head vigorously. "We are not like those wild men of Tanna. We don't eat bones.

That would be uncivilized!"

Paton stood there with his mouth hanging open. Finally he shook his head. "So you sold us one of your sacred sites for your cannibal feasts? Did you think your gods would be so offended that they would strike us dead?"

"Maybe just chase you away," said Pavingin, smiling. "But you are still here."

"That's right! And we're going to stay! You tell everyone that! Tell them that we've been digging up bones for the last hour, and nothing has harmed us."

Pavingin shrugged and walked down the hill with the other native following him.

"This may work for good," Paton said to Kevin. "When the people see we are safe, we will have proved that our God, Jehovah, is stronger than their gods."

They dug for a while longer, then Paton stopped and leaned on his shovel. "When I was on Tanna, something like this happened. The people believed that the most powerful witchcraft involved cursing something that a person was eating.

"I was preaching one day when three witch doctors stood up and told the people that Jehovah didn't have any power. They said they could kill me by casting a spell on something I'd eaten. Well, there were some plums nearby, so I took a bite out of three of them and handed them each one. Just like Elijah and the prophets of Baal in the Old Testament, I challenged them. 'Do your worst,' I said."

"Weren't you afraid?" asked Kevin.

"Of what? A god that is no god? I just mocked them. The witch doctors began their ritual to cast a spell on me, and the people became terrified, but I said, 'Be quick! Stir up your gods to help you! I'm not killed yet. In fact, I'm perfectly well.'

"Well, that went on for a whole week, and by the next Sunday they all agreed that Jehovah was the one and only true and living God! It was a great witness."

Rev. Paton went back to work, but Kevin still felt strange digging up human bones.

❖ ❖ ❖ ❖

Six weeks later the first two rooms of the Patons' house were complete, and life was much more comfortable. Kevin was beginning to get around without his crutches. His leg ached sometimes, and he still had quite a limp, but it was getting better.

The small island of Aniwa had no mountains to attract rain clouds, nor channels so that what rain did fall would collect into streams, lakes, or rivers. Therefore, during the dry season there was no source of fresh drinking water. Instead, the people drank the milk of coconuts or stagnant water from the shrinking mud holes, often making themselves sick.

Even though the island was just sandy soil that had built up—at the highest point, no more than three hundred feet above its coral reef foundation—John Paton believed fresh water was trapped below the surface. But when he suggested digging a well, the native people laughed. "Oh, Missi, don't you know? Rain comes only from above, never from the ground."

Paton started laughing.

"What did they say? What did they say?" asked Kevin. He, too, laughed when Paton translated.

"No," Paton told them. "In my country fresh water comes springing up from the ground, and I hope to see it here, too." He grabbed a shovel. "Kevin, come on. We'll show them what a well is. They have no idea. But we'd better pray that we find fresh water and not salty water that has seeped in from the sea."

After Paton and Kevin had been digging for a while, the oldest chief kindly said, "Missi, your head is going wrong. You are losing something! Don't let our people hear you talk about getting rain from below or they will never listen to your words again."

Paton translated to Kevin and then said, "Just keep digging. It will never do to argue."

"Poor Missi!" the old chief said an hour later. "That's the way they all go crazy. They get an idea in their head that won't go away. What a shame!" Then he turned to some of his younger men. "Keep watching them, and stop them if they try to take their own lives."

Kevin and Paton kept taking turns—one in the hole digging and the other above, pulling up the buckets of dirt. By afternoon, they were so tired that they could hardly climb out of the hole that was now deeper than a man with his arm extended.

"Kevin, go over to the house and bring back that bag of fishhooks. Let's see if we can buy a little labor from these chaps."

By the time Kevin returned, Paton had struck a deal: one fishhook for every three buckets of dirt they hauled up out of the well.

That worked until the next morning when they came to work. Parts of the sides of the well had caved in overnight, and none of the men would go down into the hole.

"Do you think Pavingin did this?" asked Kevin.

Paton inspected the sides and the soft sand scattered around the well. "I don't think so. I don't see any footprints or marks that anyone was trying to break the sides loose. This ground is so soft that it could easily happen on its own. We have God to thank that no one was down in there when it happened. But now what?" He scratched his beard.

"Back in Sydney, I watched them dig a well once and line it with blocks of sandstone. Why not use coral?"

"Good idea," said the missionary. "It'll be a lot of work, but . . ."

Days of grueling work resulted in a thirty-foot hole, and finally the sand began to feel damp. One evening Paton climbed out of the hole and announced, "Tomorrow I think God will give us water from that hole!" He repeated his prediction in the natives' language.

The old chief shook his head. "It won't be rain. If anything, you will drop through into the sea and be eaten by sharks!"

The next morning, in the sight of the assembled chiefs—including Pavingin—and the people, Paton prayed. Then he upended a jug. "See, it's completely empty." Then he climbed down into the well.

Kevin could hear him digging still deeper, and soon he pulled up three buckets of damp sand. Then the digging stopped, and there was silence for several minutes.

"You okay down there?" Kevin called.

"Oh yeah." There was a tone in the missionary's voice that Kevin hadn't heard before, a kind of glee. In a few minutes, Kevin heard a humming coming from the well, and then words were added.

> There shall be showers of blessing:
> This is the promise of love;
> There shall be seasons refreshing,
> Sent from the Savior above.
>
> Showers of blessing,
> Showers of blessing we need;
> Mercy-drops round us are falling,
> But for the showers we plead.

The singing stopped. "Kevin! Help me up out of here."

A minute later, John Paton was standing by the well, jug in his hand, a grin on his face, and his trouser legs wet up to his knees. He looked around at the assembled islanders, but rather than approach

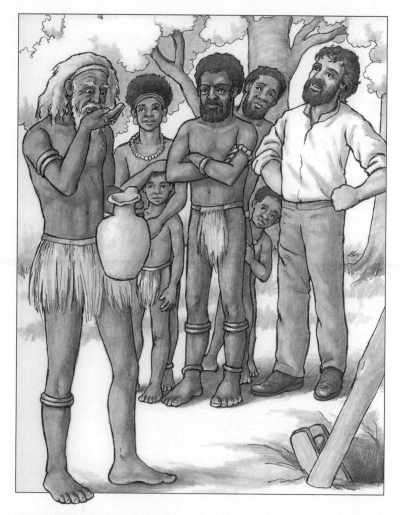

Chief Pavingin, Paton handed the jug to Chief Namakei, the oldest and most revered chief on the island. "Try this!" he said.

All gathered around as the chief shook it, spilled a little into his hands, and finally tasted it. His eyes widened. "Rain! Rain! Yes, it is rain! But how did you get it?"

"I told you," said Paton with a grin. "God gave it to us out of His own earth. Go and see for yourselves!"

"Missi," said Chief Namakei, "will you teach us that song that makes rain?"

"It's not the song. It is our good God who loves us and is eager to help us."

"Well, then, will you tell us about Him?"

Chapter 9

Back to Sea

Since it hadn't rained for a long time, the people eagerly drew water. No matter how many buckets they pulled up, the water held out and never turned salty.

On Sunday, Chief Namakei asked John Paton if he would preach to the people. When Paton agreed, Namakei called the people together. Chief Pavingin was among them, though he stood at the back of the group as the old chief spoke. "Men and women and children of Aniwa, listen to my words. Since Missi came here, he has talked many strange  things, and we thought they must be lies. But the strangest thing he said was about digging down through the earth to get rain!"

Paton translated as the old chief became more animated. "We thought he was going mad, and we mocked him, but the water was there all the same. We have laughed at other things he said because we could not see them, especially about Jehovah God. But from this day, I believe that all he says about Jehovah God is true. The gods of Aniwa cannot hear, cannot help us like the God of Missi. So today, I am ready to follow Jehovah God, and someday I will see Him with the eyes of my soul, just as Missi says."

Tears were streaming down Mrs. Paton's face when the old chief finished. "This is the beginning of the church on Aniwa," she whispered to Kevin. Kevin could hardly believe what was happening. These half-naked heathens were becoming Christians?

Rev. Paton stood and cleared his throat several times and then began to preach about Jesus. That very afternoon the old chief himself and several of his men returned to the mission house bringing the idols from their homes to be burned.

Chief Pavingin also came carrying some idols of his own. He waited until the others had thrown theirs on the fire. Then he said, "Missi Paton, when I was on Tanna, Chief Nowar put this band on my arm requiring me to protect you. I did not want to do it because the traders offered many guns if we drove you away, but Nowar made me promise.

"So I did not kill you, but I thought our gods would drive you away with magic. Now I see that they have no power, and I wish to serve Jehovah God as you have told us."

So that was it. Chief Nowar had been trying to protect the Patons all along. Kevin sighed in relief as the young chief threw his idols into the fire.

✧ ✧ ✧ ✧

Two days later, while sitting in the shade of a chestnut tree, watching Little Bob play in the sand, Kevin looked out to sea and spotted the tall white sails of a ship. He picked up the baby and ran to find Rev. Paton.

"The *Dayspring*, I think she's back!"

"Wonderful," said the missionary. "But what's the matter with you? You look like you've met yourself going the other way."

"I, well, I—" Kevin didn't know what to say. He hadn't been thinking about the *Dayspring* for some time. Suddenly he was faced with the prospect of heading back to sea. His leg was healed, and though he had been helping the Patons as much as possible, they didn't really need him any longer. The natives who had responded to the Gospel were more than willing to help the missionaries.

He shrugged. "It's just that I was . . . well, I kind of like it here on Aniwa."

"Good, that's good," said Paton. "But remember what I told you about purpose? You need to find your purpose in life, and sitting around here isn't helping you find it."

"It's just . . . going back to sea, I mean, after what happened?"

"Oh yes. You mean getting dumped overboard. That's right. You're afraid of the water, aren't you?" He pulled at his beard and then took his hat off as he sat down on a box outside the house. "Take a seat. I want to tell you something."

There was nothing handy to sit on, so Kevin sat on the ground.

"Back in Scotland," began the missionary, "when I was the pastor of Green Street Church in Glasgow, several of the elders begged me to remain there rather than come out here to the South Sea Islands. They offered me a nice house and a larger salary, but I knew God had called me. One old gentleman, however, couldn't accept my answer.

" 'But the cannibals,' he moaned, 'you'll be eaten by cannibals!'

"I wouldn't have bothered with him, except that he kept mentioning the same old warning to me, so finally I said, 'Mr. Dickson, you are old, and your body will soon be laid in its grave to be eaten by worms. What difference does it make if cannibals eat my body? Why should I save it for the worms? Isn't it more important to live and die serving and honoring the Lord Jesus?' "

John Paton stopped and sat there as though the point of his story was obvious. Finally he said, "Don't you see what I mean? Now you are young, but someday even you will die. What difference does it make whether cannibals, worms, or fish eat your body? Isn't the most important thing that you live and die serving and honoring Jesus? That's what I mean about finding your purpose. Nothing can kill you before your time, so that frees you to boldly do whatever God wants you to do."

Kevin had never thought of it that way. For a moment he caught a glimpse of this extraordinary courage, of being so sure of God's protection that you could face any danger.

The missionary continued. "Read Matthew 10:28–31 sometime, when Jesus sent His disciples out among their enemies. He told them, 'Fear not them which kill the body'—or might try to. Not even one sparrow falls to the ground apart from the Father's will. Then Jesus said, 'Fear ye not therefore, ye are of more value than many sparrows.'" Paton arched an eyebrow at Kevin. "So I think He can keep you from drowning before your time, don't you?"

Kevin looked around at the mission house, with Little Bob toddling in through the door, calling, "Mama, Mama." If John Paton could trust God for himself and his precious family in these islands where disease, accident, and cannibals threatened them every day, maybe he could trust God to keep him from drowning.

On the other hand . . . "Rev. Paton, sorry for bringing it up, but what about your first wife and child? You lost them, and you almost died then, too."

Paton leaned forward with his elbows on his knees and stared at the ground for a long time. When he finally looked up, Kevin saw tears in his eyes. "I don't know, son. Psalm 131:1 says, 'My heart is not haughty, nor mine eyes lofty: neither do I exercise myself in great matters, or in things too high for me.' I'm sure it's all right to ask God why, but if He doesn't answer, we need to let God be God. He might have reasons we can't understand."

Paton stood up and put his hat back on. "In any case, as you see, I *did* come back. I'm still trusting Him to keep me until *my* time. Come on, let's go meet that ship."

✧ ✧ ✧ ✧

Kevin was sad to leave Aniwa. Back at sea on the *Dayspring*, he often thought of that conversation and the courage John Paton had described that came from trusting God. But when a storm kicked up, his stomach still tightened into a knot. He didn't actually get sick and lose his last meal, but he found himself hanging on extra tight to the ropes and railings on the deck.

Was he just a coward? What did it mean to trust God when he was scared? Somewhere he remembered a Bible story about not tempting God with foolish actions . . . oh yeah, Jesus said it when Satan dared Him to jump off the temple tower. Okay, so trusting God didn't mean being reckless, he reminded himself. Kevin held on tight and inched his way across the pitching deck with sea spray blowing in his face. He'd do his job, but he'd be careful and hope God would take care of the rest.

Life settled into a routine of visiting island after island to bring supplies to the missionaries or ferry the missionaries to the headquarters in Anatom. Kevin began to feel comfortable with his new life.

Twice they encountered the *Hopeful* with Williams and McNeil aboard. Once they passed it while they were at sea, but neither ship exchanged greetings. The other time they arrived at an island just as the *Hopeful* was sailing away. On the beach were about thirty people, wailing and throwing themselves on the sand—family members of slaves who had been taken away on the *Hopeful*. The people comforted themselves with the white traders' assurances that their relatives would return in a couple years.

"Imagine how they would grieve," muttered Mr. Samson as they returned to the *Dayspring*, "if they knew that most of their loved ones will die within the next two years from overwork, lack of food, and beatings. Even those who survive plantation life may never find a ride back to this island. In all likelihood they are gone forever."

"Why don't we go after them?" asked Kevin. He had visions of returning the slaves in triumph.

Captain Fraser, who was standing by, said, "We're not a man-o'-war. How could we force them to surrender the natives?"

Kevin's shoulders sagged. Frustrated, he went back down into the hold to finish rearranging the barrels of supplies for their next stop.

✧ ✧ ✧

Shortly after the New Year, the *Dayspring* returned to the mission headquarters on the Island of Anatom. It anchored in the bay as usual, out beyond the coral reef that guarded the shore. Most of the crew went ashore for a rest. Each morning, a couple men would row the longboat out to the ship and relieve the two sailors who stayed on board so they could take their turn ashore.

After taking his turn on the *Dayspring*, Kevin came ashore on Sunday morning, January 5, just in time for worship. Church services on Anatom were more like what he had experienced back in Sydney. Not only were several missionaries in attendance, but most of the natives on the island had become Christians, so the singing was joyful, and some of the preaching was in English.

But during the service, Kevin noticed another sound: the whine of wind and heavy rain. As they came out of the little chapel, a tremendous storm was developing. It looked like it was going to be the first hurricane of the season.

Already the rain drove sideways, and waves taller than a man rolled across the reef, into the beach, and up among the palm trees that whipped around in the wind like the tails on a hundred cats.

"Two men are still out there on the *Dayspring*," Captain Fraser yelled at Kevin as he went running down toward the beach. "We gotta row out and rescue 'em." He grabbed Kevin by the arm and pulled him toward the longboat. Mr. Samson and two other sailors came along behind carrying huge coils of rope.

The longboat was lashed with ropes to several trees, but every time a large wave came flooding up onto the shore, it was jerked nearly free. All five of the crew members were bruised and battered by the bucking boat before they got it launched. Keeping the boat headed straight into the huge breakers so it would not be rolled over proved harder than rowing up a raging river.

Finally the longboat crossed the reef and moved to within a hundred feet of the *Dayspring*. But suddenly a huge gust of wind broke both masts off the

ship. The rescuers could see that no one on board was hurt, but the masts and rigging floating in a tangled mess made approaching the ship as difficult as rowing through a fishing net. Fortunately, Kevin was so busy with the rescue efforts that he had no time to think about his own fears. Getting the men off the ship while the waves butted the longboat into the hull of the larger ship like an angry billy goat exhausted everyone.

Two hours later, with the sky as dark as the sea, they finally skidded the longboat safely to a stop on the scoured beach.

When Kevin climbed over the side, his legs felt so weak that he slumped to the sand after no more than a dozen steps toward the tree line. He just sat in the driving wind, rain, and spray, looking back out at the tattered remains of the *Dayspring*. Would they ever be able to fix her?

Captain Fraser slapped his shoulder. "Come on, son," he yelled, "get out of this weather. If one of those big waves doesn't snatch you away, you'll catch your death of cold."

"But look!" yelled Kevin. "She's . . . she's movin'. The storm's driving her closer!"

"Mr. Samson," yelled Captain Fraser. Soon all the crew were huddled together on the beach, peering out through the gloom. "Do you think she's dragging her anchor?"

"Looks that way," said the first mate.

Finally, Captain Fraser said, "Well, if she's dragging her anchor, there's nothing we can do but pray.

We don't have an extra anchor, and even if we did, there's no going back out there now."

They all stared for a few more moments. "Yep. She's movin'. She'll be on the reef before dark. But there's nothin' to be done! We'd all lose our lives tryin'. Let's go in."

With what felt like a stone in his stomach, Kevin followed the others to the mission compound. One last time he looked back through the raging storm for a glimpse of *his* ship. The pouch containing the printed *Dayspring* shares hung from his neck, but all he could see was the ghost of a hull pitching and rolling over the turbulent waves.

Chapter 10

The Derelict Dwelling

The next morning everyone's worst fears were realized. There was no *Dayspring* floating in the now peaceful bay of Anatom. With the help of some of the native boys who were good divers, Captain Fraser took the longboat out to see if they could find the sunken remains of the ship.

There was no trace.

"Do you suppose she drifted out to sea?" asked Kevin.

Mr. Samson searched the horizon. "Not much chance, really. The wind was blowing her toward shore. But what I can't figure is why the beach isn't strewn with wreckage."

"Maybe the wind changed during

the night and blew her out to sea. Do you think that's possible, Mr. Samson?"

"Well, my boy, anything's possible when it comes to the sea. But it doesn't seem likely to me."

About an hour later they noticed two native canoes coming along the shore from the west. The men were pulling hard on their paddles, and they were yelling something to the sailors who were still sitting around on the beach, shocked at the loss of their ship.

As the canoes drew closer, Kevin finally figured out what the men were yelling. Jumping to his feet, Kevin said, "It's the *Dayspring*." His young ears had heard what the older men couldn't hear. "They're saying, 'Missi's ship! Missi's ship! Missi's ship!' "

In moments the whole crew of the *Dayspring* was down to the water's edge, waiting to receive the excited natives.

As the canoes slid onto the beach and the men jumped out, gesturing back the way they had come, they tried to tell their story. It was about a ship.

"Kevin," said Captain Fraser, "run and get one of the missionaries who can translate what these fellows are trying to say."

When Kevin returned with someone who could translate, they discovered that the natives had found the wreck of the *Dayspring* stranded high on the sand, two miles west.

With high hopes that their beloved ship was safe, they ran down the beach. Soon the sailors and natives were strung out like a cross-country race. Kevin managed to keep up with most of the natives, but the sailors dropped behind, with the older Captain Fraser bringing up the rear.

Kevin rounded a sand dune and saw the dark hull of the ship in the distance. It tipped to one side slightly, but otherwise it didn't look too bad. The masts were missing, of course. But that had happened before it started dragging its anchor. They could be replaced.

Hope rose in his heart even while his lungs cried for mercy from such a long run. Then his pace slowed as he approached until he was walking, getting a good look at the stranded vessel.

Rigging hung from the side and stretched out across the sand like dark spider webs. The rudder was broken off, but that, too, could be replaced. And then Kevin saw it . . . a huge, gaping hole in the side of the once proud ship. He walked even slower as he approached. The hole was as tall as a man. The barrels he'd been adjusting just a couple days before could be seen. A flicker of pride crossed his mind: He had tied them securely. But the ship . . .

By then the other sailors, Mr. Samson, and finally Captain Fraser were approaching. They walked around the hull, looking up at the damage in silence, sometimes reaching out to touch the hull.

Kevin slapped the side of the ship. "She'll sail again, don't you think, Captain?"

The captain had picked up a stout stick and was pushing the tip in between the planks in the ship's side. He moved it back and forth like a crowbar.

"What are you doing, sir?" said one of the sailors.

"We don't want to tear any more planks loose, do we?"

No sooner had the sailor said the words, than the end of a plank sprang out from the side of the ship. The captain threw the stick to the ground in disgust. "She's not seaworthy, lads." He reached down and picked up the stick again. "Look here, all along here. It's not the hole in her side—we could fix that—and it's not just the rudder or the masts and rigging. We could replace all that. But look here. She's taken such a beating that she's coming apart at the seams. I wouldn't trust her in a blow a mile from shore. Just like that plank right there, she could start coming apart in a heavy sea, and we wouldn't be able to do a thing but ride her to the bottom. Her seagoing days are over."

Everyone stood around in sullen silence until one of the sailors climbed into the hull through the hole in her side. "I'm just going to get my stuff." Soon the others followed, but Kevin stayed outside.

He sat on the sand with head hanging low. Around his neck was the pouch with the shares inside. What were they worth now? Nothing. He got them out and counted them like money. When the captain came around the bow of the ship again, Kevin looked up and said, "Captain Fraser, who's she belong to now?"

"The *Dayspring*? I think the sea's claimed her, as it does all ships sooner or later. I'll file an insurance report, and maybe John Paton and the mission agency can collect something on her, but as far as this pile of timbers is concerned, she's just a derelict.

She'll stay here until the weather beats her into driftwood, scattered on the shores of the seven seas. Like I said, she belongs to the sea now."

Within an hour, the *Dayspring*'s crew and the natives who had found her drifted back up the beach by twos and threes toward the mission headquarters, but Kevin remained behind, sitting in the shade of the derelict, counting his shares of "nothing."

What was he to do now? What *could* he do? He didn't want to go back to Sydney. He didn't want to find a berth on some other ship. Life on other ships could be cruel—maybe worse than a sheep station in Australia's wilderness.

Hunger finally urged him to return to the mission station.

✧ ✧ ✧ ✧

Days passed at the mission station as the captain and the other missionaries tried to figure out what should be done. Maybe they could lease another ship for a while until the *Dayspring* could be replaced. But the whole idea held no attraction for Kevin. His ship, the one in which he was part owner, was finished.

One afternoon, without anything better to do, he walked down the beach. Seeing the *Dayspring* in the distance, so isolated and stark on the white sand, gave him an eerie feeling. He missed his days at sea. The *Dayspring* had become his home, and now he was homeless. . . . Or was he?

The closer he got to the old wreck, the more an idea grew in his mind. He stepped through the hole in its side and climbed up onto the slanting deck. He walked around recalling the old days. It had been a good home. Why not make it his home again?

Yes, why not? It was better than nothing, and he had nothing better to do. He would make the *Dayspring* his home. Even if it wasn't seaworthy, it was still as solid as any house on the island. And it was as much his as anyone else's—maybe more. After all, he still had his shares declaring him to be part owner. Everyone else had abandoned the old derelict as worthless. Why couldn't he claim it?

He made his way down into the galley. The stove was sitting at such an angle that it would be hard to boil water, but he could level it by propping up the low side.

Looking like an old cargo net, his rope hammock still hung from the beam. Sand and dried seaweed was everywhere, but he could clean out all that. There were coconut and other fruit trees nearby. He could fish and live like a native. It would be an adventure, certainly better than being sent to a sheep station, and maybe even better than going to sea.

For the first time since the hurricane, Kevin began taking interest in life. He cleaned and swept and sorted the remaining supplies. The seawater had destroyed many things, but some items of value remained, even some sealed tins of biscuits and a large bag of limes.

That evening he built a fire on the sand near the

hole into the hull—the door to his house, as he now thought of it. The tide had risen until waves lapped gently against the far side of the *Dayspring*'s hull. Kevin wondered for a while whether the water would come around and put out his fire, but he didn't worry. So what? The night sky was clear, and he felt free again as he looked up at the stars. There was time enough to think about his future and his purpose in life, as John Paton had urged him to do. For right now, he would enjoy his mansion by the sea. After all, it was larger than any house he had ever been in.

The next day some of the Christian natives from the island stopped by and shared food with Kevin. They'd seen his fire the night before and were curious.

"Alone not good! Alone not good for boy," said the one who spoke the most English. "You come to mission house."

Kevin smiled broadly. It was nice of them to be so concerned, but he shook his head and pointed toward the *Dayspring*. "No, this is my home! This is home . . . house!"

However, after a couple of days, he realized that his "house" had a serious problem. He climbed up on the deck and searched the shoreline for as far as he could see. Then he looked out to sea. "Water, water, everywhere, Nor any drop to drink." It was a line from a poem that his mother used to quote, "The Rime of the Ancient Mariner" by Samuel Taylor Coleridge, as Kevin remembered. But it would soon be true enough for him, too. There had only been one

small water cask on board the ship that hadn't broken open and was still fresh. And he had already used most of it.

Then he had an idea. He went back down into the ship's hull and broke open a barrel that had been intended for missionaries. Inside were clothes of all sorts. That afternoon when some natives came by, he brought an armload out and began holding the garments up in front of himself to demonstrate how they were to be worn. "Trade clothes for water. Clothes for water. You bring water."

But for some reason, the natives weren't interested in trading. "No. You come get water from the stream," they urged. "Much water. You take it, all you want." So Kevin grabbed a small keg and followed them inland. It was more than a mile over steep sand dunes before they arrived at the stream. The water was rather cloudy, but it was fresh. He filled the keg, but five gallons of water weighed far more than he imagined once he started trudging back over the sand dunes. He had to find a better solution.

What he needed was some kind of cart, one with wheels that wouldn't sink too far into the sand. The only place where he might get something like that was the mission station, but Kevin didn't know how he'd be welcomed there. He had half expected Captain Fraser or Mr. Samson to come looking for him. Did they consider him a runaway—or a deserter? Would they try to send him back to Sydney? He just didn't know. Then one day he finally worked up the courage to return.

Captain Fraser and the crew of the *Dayspring* were not there. They had caught a ride on a passing trading ship to Sydney, hoping to find some other vessel to use for mission work. "Captain Fraser said to tell you he'd be back." The other missionaries seemed glad enough to see him. They'd heard from the Christian natives where he was living and didn't seem worried—just wanted to know how he was managing. Kevin was surprised that no one bawled him out or tried to tell him what to do. But he was pleased to know he could keep living in the *Dayspring* and come and go at the mission when he wanted. He even found a couple old baby-buggy wheels from which to make a cart for his water kegs.

Day after day went by as Kevin worked hard to "make a living" on the beach. But one morning he was awakened by the sound of voices outside. Someone began banging on the hull.

"Well, well," mocked a gruff voice, "I said I'd see this boat on the bottom of the sea before I'd tolerate any more interference from those missionaries. Guess someone has saved me the trouble."

"Hey, someone's been building a fire here," came another voice—one Kevin remembered, but to whom did it belong? "Those cannibals probably come down here to cook their enemies. Better watch out, McNeil, or they'll roast you for dinner."

McNeil? Agent McNeil? It couldn't be, but—

"Let 'em try," came the first voice again. "I'm too tough. They'd have to find a big pot and boil me all night. Even then I'd give 'em indigestion."

Several men laughed.

Kevin quietly climbed up the steps until his head emerged above the deck, and a fresh sea breeze ruffled his hair. He couldn't see who was standing below on the beach outside his ship, but when he looked out to sea, there sat the *Hopeful*, anchored just beyond the reef.

Chapter 11

A Slave to the Traders

L et's start stripping her." It was Williams' voice. "I want all the brass, any rigging, the compass, extra sails, nails—anything of value. Okay, get to work, men!"

Stripping his house? Kevin couldn't let that happen. But what could he do against several men? He clasped the pouch of shares that he still wore around his neck. This was his ship. He had the papers to prove it—at least it was his if the mission didn't want it. And the mission hadn't made any attempt to salvage it.

The mission—he had to escape to the mission and get help. If he could just get away and run up the beach, some of the missionaries would surely come to his aid and prevent the traders from ruining his house.

Staying low as he crawled across the deck, Kevin looked down to the damp sand on the seaward side. If he could climb down and run straight into the water while the traders busied themselves on the other side of the ship, maybe they wouldn't notice him. But what would he do when he got in the water?

If he could only swim, he would swim parallel to the beach toward the mission station. He should have learned to swim. Some of the native boys would have gladly taught him. They were good swimmers. But that old fear of the water kept him away. Now he needed the skill.

Then he happened to notice the traders' longboat beached at the water's edge. It was a large rowboat, pretty heavy for one person to handle, but the stern rose a few inches with each small wave that broke beneath it. They hadn't pulled it very far onto the sand. If he could just get to it without their seeing him, maybe he could hide on the other side while he worked it loose and pulled it into the water, where he could jump in and row for help.

"Hey, it looks like someone's been living in here," came a voice within the hull.

Kevin knew he had very little time before the traders found him. He threw a rope from the tattered rigging over the side, made it secure, and climbed down. When he hit the sand, he took one glance to either side and raced for the longboat.

In three splashes through the water he was

around to the stern, crouching out of sight. Now, if he could just pull the boat free from the sand without anyone seeing him. He gave a yank—no success. He tried again, timing his effort with the next small wave that lifted the stern. He gained a couple inches. He did it with the next wave, and the next.

Suddenly the boat was drifting free. He backed up as the water got deeper and deeper until it was up to his armpits. Then he heaved himself up over the stern and rolled into the bottom of the boat, remaining quiet and listening for a shout of alarm from shore.

No one yelled. No one came running to stop him. They were too busy exploring the loot they had found in the *Dayspring*.

Kevin sat up, got into position, and took up two oars. He pulled three strokes when he heard a tremendous explosion from somewhere behind him. He turned just in time to see a puff of white smoke mushrooming from the bow of the *Hopeful*.

They had fired a cannon! They couldn't be shooting at him, could they? What were they doing?

In ten seconds, Kevin found out. The men on the *Hopeful* had seen Kevin and fired a signal shot to the men on shore. Kevin turned just in time to see three traders come onto the deck of the *Dayspring*. In an instant they saw that he was stealing their longboat. One came over the side by the same rope Kevin had used. The other two went back down into the hold, yelling for assistance from their comrades.

Before the longboat plowed into the next small

wave, six men were running toward the water, yelling and waving their hands as they splashed into the surf.

Kevin pulled harder. If only he could get out into deep water, he'd have a chance. Hadn't Captain Fraser said very few seagoing men knew how to swim? Hadn't he said that they didn't even want to learn? But as he watched, Williams and one of the sailors kept coming until they were waist deep. Then they dove in and swam right toward him.

He had thirty feet on them, but they were gaining. The old boat was just too heavy to outrun them. In no time, they had grabbed the gunwales and were coming up and over the side. Kevin made one feeble effort to fight them off with an oar, but it was no use.

"What do you think you're doing, you little thief?" bellowed Williams, water streaming down his angry face as he grasped Kevin by the shirt and yanked him up.

Kevin thought the angry traders were going to throw him over the side right there, but instead they threw him onto the bottom of the boat and sat down, gasping for breath after their quick swim.

Kevin lay there feeling hopeless and foolish as they turned the boat around and rowed back to shore.

"What do you think you were going to do with our boat?" yelled Agent McNeil when Williams had beached the longboat again.

"I was going for help. This is my ship," said Kevin, drawing on all his courage. He wasn't going to give up without a fight. "You have no right to strip it."

"*Your* ship? Ha! What makes you think it is your ship?"

Kevin flipped the thong over his head and held his pouch out in front of him. "I'm a shareholder, the only one who's bothered to stay with the ship. So it's mine. Everyone else has abandoned it."

McNeil snatched the pouch and tossed it to the side. "It's an abandoned derelict. You don't count. We're just claiming the rights of salvage."

"You can't do that!" In desperation Kevin said, "It . . . it might go to sea again someday!"

"To sea? You think this thing'll float? Did you miss that big hole in the side you've been walking through?"

"Well, it could be fixed! Even Captain Fraser said the hole could be repaired, and she could be fitted with a new rudder and . . . and new masts. She'll sail again!"

"Not if I have anything to say about it. We're going to strip her, and then we're going to burn her. What do you think about that?"

"Wait a minute." Williams had taken his shirt off and was wringing the water out of it. "The kid might have a point. What if *we* patched her up?"

"You think I'm going to be caught in that leaky tub halfway between here and Australia?" McNeil dismissed Williams with a wave of his hand. "You're crazy!"

"No, no. Listen to me. We don't have to take her out in the open sea very far. We have the *Hopeful* for that, but between the islands—listen, the natives are starting to run from us when we drop anchor. But with the *Dayspring* they would come to us! See?"

"You mean they would think we were the missionaries and welcome us? Then . . ." McNeil left his meaning hanging.

Williams' sneer widened. "Right."

McNeil glanced at Kevin. "What about the kid? We don't want him telling those missionaries or word's liable to get around, and the natives won't trust us."

"Yeah. The kid." Williams shook out his shirt and put it back on. "Well, since he thinks he's the *owner* 'cause he stuck with the ship, maybe we should just keep him on. This can be an 'owner-run' ship. He can do all the work!"

All the traders broke up laughing.

Kevin walked over and retrieved his pouch, but what difference did it make? The traders intended to make him their slave! This couldn't be happening. He would have been better off on a sheep station.

❖ ❖ ❖ ❖

In the days that followed, Kevin was forced to work harder than he had ever worked in his life. While McNeil and Williams and some of the other men patched the hull and repaired the rudder, Kevin dug trenches and cut and hauled logs. They dug under the ship to place logs like tracks down to the water. Then they cut smaller logs to serve as rollers to move the ship down into the water.

After two weeks of torturous work from dawn to dark they succeeded in floating the *Dayspring*. Kevin thought he would get a break, but the old ship leaked so badly that he was forced to help man the pump several hours a day while the traders cut and erected new masts and rigged the ship.

Dropping to the deck with exhaustion one evening, he wondered why they hadn't rigged the ship while it was still in "dry dock." At least then he wouldn't have had to put in so much work pumping out the seawater. The sailors were making some effort to plug the leaks with fresh oakum, but it was in short supply.

Kevin was too tired to make his way below deck to get something to eat, and he soon fell asleep curled up in the bow of the ship.

When he awoke several hours later, no one was on deck. A small light could be seen on the deck of the *Hopeful* a hundred yards away on the other side of the reef, but only the moon illumined the *Dayspring*. Kevin walked to the side of the ship and looked toward the beach.

The white sand and small waves that broke onto it seemed powdered with moon dust. It was a beautiful sight, and it wasn't that far away. Kevin looked down; if he could only swim, he could make it to shore and run for freedom.

Why hadn't any missionaries come to rescue him? Surely the natives had noticed all the work being done to the *Dayspring* and told the missionaries. Why hadn't someone come to investigate? Did they know *who* was salvaging the *Dayspring*? Did they know what it would mean to the natives? Did they think he was taking part willingly? Or were they just too busy to be checking up on him?

For the first time since he had made the *Dayspring* his home, Kevin felt truly alone.

The next morning at high tide, Williams planned to take the *Dayspring* out through a narrow passage in the coral reef that he hoped was wide enough. But was it? If they hit the coral, no telling what would happen. On the other hand, if they made it out successfully, Kevin would be their captive.

This was his last chance to escape, but the only way was to swim for it. He began to shake as he faced the prospect of going into the water again. He tried to remind himself of Rev. Paton's words that nothing could harm him before his time, especially while he was doing God's work, but he just couldn't muster up the courage. He couldn't take the plunge!

Chapter 12

Coral Reef Relief

Williams' scheme for using the *Dayspring* to fool the island people worked all too well. After sailing the former missionary ship through the coral reef that guarded the southern coast of Anatom, the *Dayspring* visited many islands in the New Hebrides where the missionaries' ship had been known.

In each instance, islanders came paddling out to welcome the missionaries. The traders greeted them with small gifts and did everything they could to maintain a pretense as missionaries, sometimes even singing songs—though they were usually barroom songs rather than Christian songs.

"Sing hearty, lads," McNeil yelled one morning when they

dropped anchor in a bay and were surrounded by islanders in their canoes. "These cannibals won't know the difference."

Kevin hung back, sick at heart that "his" ship was now being used in such an ugly trade. He noticed that the traders were careful to kidnap only two or three natives from each island and only when others were not around to observe. It was a sly attempt to maintain their disguise. They quickly gagged and hid their captives below deck until they were away from the island. Then they transferred their captives to the *Hopeful* for the trip to the plantations in Australia.

Kevin was just as much a slave as the poor islanders. But one day when the *Dayspring* had dropped anchor and native canoes were approaching, McNeil yelled, "Boy, get up on deck and show yourself."

Show himself? Standing at the ship's railing, Kevin suddenly realized that he, too, was part of the deception. The traders hoped that the natives would recognize him and be further reassured that it was the missionary ship. He couldn't let that happen.

As the canoes came closer, Kevin started yelling. "Go back! Go back! This is not Missi's ship! Flee for your lives—"

✧ ✧ ✧ ✧

Light as warm as his mother's hearth fire glowed through his eyelids. But when he tried to open them, it was like lifting sacks of flour, revealing the searing

125

glare of noonday sun. His head throbbed like the steam engine on a Sydney ferry, each chug white-hot pain.

He looked up at the ship's rigging swaying across the sky. He must still be on the *Dayspring*. But why was he on his back on the deck? Slowly he sat up, rubbing the huge, painful lump on the back of his head.

"Try that little trick again, and you'll wish you were dinner for those cannibals," snarled McNeil. "That's mutiny, as far as I'm concerned. I won't put up with it! You understand that?"

Kevin leaned forward with his head in his hands and mumbled, "How can it be mutiny when I never signed on with you? You're holdin' me against my will. If you tried to bring charges, I'd tell the court—"

"You won't tell a court nothin'! You'll never see a court! I run this ship, and my word goes." He stopped, his face contorted with rage. After a moment, he added with a sneer, "Besides, you were the one who claimed this was your ship. We're just along for the ride, ain't that right, lads?"

Several of the sailors laughed.

After that, Kevin looked for a chance to escape at every island they visited, but the traders watched him closely whenever the natives brought their canoes alongside the ship, and his old fear of the water prevented him from jumping ship and trying to swim for shore when they weren't on guard. *Besides*, he reminded himself whenever he looked toward a welcoming beach, *I still haven't learned how to swim.*

✧ ✧ ✧

Once the *Hopeful* had as many slaves as it could hold, Williams and a few of his men sailed it for Australia. McNeil then anchored the *Dayspring* offshore from an island Kevin had never seen. It was surrounded by reefs similar to Aniwa, but this time the traders made no attempt to conceal their identity from the islanders.

Canoes came out over the reef and welcomed the ship. And the sailors began talking about having a feast on shore. After listening closely, Kevin discovered that the main chief on this island was a partner of the traders. He knew about their slave trading. In fact, he regularly delivered his prisoners of war to them.

"Those prisoners are lucky," said one sailor. "We're actually saving their lives. Before we came along, they would have been eaten." He laughed. "Now they get to go to Australia. Who knows, some of them might get civilized . . . if they survive." More laughter.

Soon the traders climbed into their longboat and headed toward the island amid the canoes. Kevin was left alone on the *Dayspring*.

As the afternoon passed, clouds came up and the wind increased, swinging the ship around so that its stern was toward the island while it tugged at its anchor. Kevin finally ventured into Williams' cabin and found his telescope and went to the rear of the *Dayspring* to see what was happening on shore. There was certainly a great party in progress on the beach, but as the wind increased, he watched the drunken revelers begin moving inland to the village huts that were just visible through the trees. Their longboat remained abandoned on the beach. Had the traders forgotten their ship and the rising storm?

As the *Dayspring* rolled with the growing waves, Kevin began to worry. This was not the strongest ship anymore. What if she began to break apart? He walked the now pitching deck of the *Dayspring*. The sails were securely furled. The boom and the rudder were tied down. The forward hatch was closed. He went below and closed the doors to all the cabins. Everything seemed shipshape, or at least as good as could be expected for a salvaged wreck in the care of these careless traders.

Back topside the storm had so darkened the afternoon sky that Kevin was inclined to light a couple lanterns. But why? No other ship was near. And the traders would be partying all night. What did he care whether they thought he was "on duty" or not? But lanterns would lend some comfort in the growing storm. He lit one for the stern and then carried a second one forward to hang from the bowsprit.

While hanging it from the bowsprit, he noticed how the *Dayspring* was straining at the anchor rope. What if she began to drag her anchor as she had done once before? He watched it as the thick rope creaked and vibrated from the tension. A particularly large wave broke against the side of the ship, drenching Kevin with spray.

If that anchor didn't hold, the ship would soon crash into the treacherous reef. He knew from experience how sharp the coral could be. His leg ached

just thinking about it. Kevin looked back over his shoulder. The waves were crashing with tremendous fury across the reef. The weakened *Dayspring* would be smashed to splinters.

Kevin tried to calm himself. This was a big blow, but it was no hurricane. He should just trust the anchor. Everything would be okay.

He walked to the back of the ship, weaving with the roll of its deck, and stared at the waves breaking over the reef. It sure would crush a ship to be battered against it. Forgetting himself for a moment, Kevin thought that would sure serve these traders right. They had stolen "his" *Dayspring* and made him a slave in their evil scheme of kidnapping the very people the ship was intended to serve. He stood in a daze, hanging on to the railing as he imagined his ship drifting across the fifty yards of churning water until it crunched into the reef.

In his mind's eye, he saw it leaning to one side, taking on water through a new hole. Without its normal buoyancy, it would crash harder and harder into the reef with each successive wave. Finally, one wave too many would cause it to capsize, and then the next one would roll it over. The masts would break. The sides would crush, and then it would turn to splinters . . . but those "splinters" would be huge timbers flipping into the air like matchsticks.

And that would be the end!

Spray hit Kevin in the face and shook him out of his daydream. The ship was rolling beneath him, but the anchor still held.

On the other hand, the end of the *Dayspring* would stop the traders' evil scheme.

Kevin opened the pouch that hung around his neck. In the gray light, he studied the top share. *This certificate entitles you to one share ownership in the missionary ship* Dayspring. At the bottom were the words, *You are helping bring the Gospel to those who have never heard.* But the *Dayspring* was no longer bringing "good news" to anyone.

Kevin flipped through the certificates. He had a hundred of them. If he was really one of the owners, he had a responsibility for how his ship was used.

The image of the *Dayspring* tumbling over the reef like matchsticks burned in his mind. That would be better than its current use.

Hanging on to the railing like a drunken man, he walked to the front of the ship and stared again at the taut anchor rope. There was an ax in the carpenter's chest just below deck. He could get it. He could use it to cut the anchor rope, and the *Dayspring* would never again be used to enslave the islands' people.

But he would drown in the process.

John Paton had said, *"What difference does it make whether cannibals, worms, or fish eat your body?"* Had God put him here to stop a great evil? Oh, but . . . drowning! It was the thing Kevin feared most.

And yet sinking the *Dayspring* had to be done. Could he trust God to care for him while he was doing what had to be done? He looked out at the sea. Even if he were a good swimmer, the chance of making it to shore was almost impossible in weather like this. Maybe this was just his time. Jesus had said not even one sparrow falls to the ground apart from the Father's will. Could he trust God to make that decision for his life?

Kevin went back and opened the front hatch. It was dark below deck, but he knew where the carpenter's chest was and went right to it. Suddenly something hit him in the legs. He stumbled and fell. It hit him again. For an instant Kevin thought someone else was still on the ship and had attacked him, and then he realized that he had just tripped over an old water keg, empty and rolling around in the hold. How had it gotten loose? Kevin picked himself up and opened the carpenter's chest and removed the ax.

Then he had an idea. An empty barrel would float. It would float very well. It might float high enough to carry him *over* the reef and take him all the way to shore . . . if there were a way to hold on to it in the churning water. How could he hang on? He needed handles. . . . His hammock! He could wrap his rope hammock around the barrel and tie it securely. The cords would give him many handholds, secure enough that a wave would not yank the keg from him. All he'd have to do would be to hang on.

It might work! It just might work!

He grabbed the keg with one arm and the ax with the other hand and hurried up on the deck. Whatever he did, he'd have to do it before dark. He went below again and got his hammock. Back on deck he tied it around the barrel and checked his grip. He decided that before he jumped into the water, he would tie one of the cords from his hammock around his wrist. If he somehow let go of the keg, it could not drift far away.

Then he went forward and stood with ax in hand above the anchor rope that came through the gunwale and stretched, tight as a drum, across the deck to the capstan.

Chapter 13

The *Dayspring II*

Kevin's first chop bounced off the wrist-thick anchor rope, leaving only a small scar. He looked over his shoulder toward the island as though one of the traders might see what he was doing, but there was no one on the beach.

He swung again and again. With each solid hit, strands of tough cord snapped apart. Fearing the end of the rope would whip back and break his leg, Kevin moved as far away as possible for his final swing. *Wang!* One end whipped across the deck while the other snaked through the hole in the gunwale and into the sea.

The *Dayspring* was adrift.

Kevin grabbed up his flotation keg and attached a free rope to his wrist.

133

Now the question was, from which side of the ship should he jump? He didn't want to be in the path of the ship when it drifted into the reef. And he didn't want to get there after the crash. The timbers and wreckage bobbing around in the waves could be dangerous.

But there was no time for such calculation. He had to make his move without delay. Holding on to the rigging to steady himself, he stepped up onto the portside railing, took a deep breath as he hugged the small barrel, and jumped!

Ker-splush!

The barrel was yanked from his arms as it remained on the surface while his momentum drove him under. He had been smart to tie the rope around his wrist. He held his breath and pulled himself to the surface beside his barrel.

He gasped for breath and grabbed a handful of net around the barrel, trying to pull himself up. The barrel spun, and he went under. Up he came and frantically tried it again. His flotation device was not keeping him up. Again, the barrel spun as he tried to pull himself up onto it, and he went under.

When he came up, he was coughing and had to get his breath before trying to grab the top of the barrel again. And then suddenly he realized that the barrel was keeping his head above water. The trick was to hold on to the ropes at the *bottom* so that when he pushed down, it wouldn't spin.

It still took some trial and error, because the barrel always had a tendency to be on top with him below, and that put his head under water. But he finally got the knack.

He looked around. Where was the ship? The wind had caught it and was moving it toward the reef. Good! He needed to keep as much distance as possible between himself and the ship. He didn't want to get tangled up in its wreckage. But he did want to get over the reef. He spotted a point where the waves were rolling rather than breaking and decided that the water must be deeper and safer there.

Kevin knew swimming required kicking, so he tried, and though the going was very slow, he was able to move himself toward the safer point in the reef. For several minutes he kicked in that direction. And then he heard a great crunch and looked over to see the *Dayspring* colliding with the reef. Just as he had imagined, each wave smashed its side into the sharp underwater coral.

For a moment, Kevin thought that the next big wave might lift it right over the reef into the safety of calm water. That would defeat his plans. The traders would just repair the damage and find a way to get the ship back out into the open sea. But then the next wave drove it hard into the reef, causing the ship to tip far to one side. He heard loud cracks and pops as the planking gave way, and when the wave had passed and the ship settled back, Kevin could see that it was taking on water and floating much lower.

The following waves brought more and more damage until, just like he had imagined, it was no more

than a pile of timbers, rigging, and masts tumbling over and over.

At that moment, Kevin felt a wave lifting him higher than usual. He was at the reef. He pulled his legs up, remembering the pain of the sharp coral. In a moment he was on the foaming crest, looking down the far side of the wave into the lagoon. Then he was sliding down it.

Holding tightly to his barrel, he made it safely over.

✧ ✧ ✧ ✧

Kevin peered out from the thicket where he had been hiding on the island, and his heart leaped. For five days he had wondered about his fate: Would

McNeil find him? The cannibals? Or would he starve to death? But dropping anchor on the other side of the reef was a large British warship. Within an hour the captain and ten men were rowing to shore. Throwing caution to the wind, Kevin left his hiding spot and ran down to the beach, begging for their protection.

It wasn't just any captain who had come ashore in that longboat. Sir William Wiseman was commodore of the HMS *Curaçoa*, the British man-o'-war that had been searching the New Hebrides islands for McNeil and Williams and their deceiving vessels.

The commodore scowled as he listened to Kevin's story. "That's a pretty tall tale, son. You mean to tell me that you sank their ship all by yourself?"

"Yes, sir. But the *Dayspring* didn't really belong to the traders. In fact, it was my—" Kevin stopped, realizing how unlikely it would sound to claim that he owned a ship. "Look, there's the *Dayspring*'s longboat right down the beach, and there's some of the wreckage. Doesn't that prove my story?"

"Maybe."

"But McNeil and some of his men are still on the island. I've been afraid that they'd find me, but they couldn't have escaped. No other ship has been by."

The commodore's sharp eyes studied Kevin. "Lieutenant, take a detail and search the island. See if you can turn up this McNeil and his men. Be quick about it."

Two hours later, a subdued McNeil and four of his men stood in irons before the commodore. The slave trader stared in astonishment at Kevin, then hatred hooded his eyes. *He thought I was dead when the* Dayspring *sank*, Kevin realized.

"Well, young man," the British officer said as the soldiers took the prisoners out to the ship, "looks like your story proved true. Your testimony in court will go a long way toward convicting these scoundrels. They'll never bother you or the natives of these islands again."

When Kevin hauled himself over the railing of the HMS *Curaçoa* for the short trip to Anatom, his eyes widened. The man-o'-war was huge compared to the *Dayspring*.

When the big warship anchored in the bay of the island that held the mission headquarters, Kevin noticed another ship at anchor, a three-masted ship he had never seen before. It was slightly larger than the *Dayspring*, and the name on the side read *Paragon*. On shore he was surprised to see John Paton and most of the other missionaries from the islands coming down to the shore to welcome the visitors. They had gathered again for their annual meeting. Captain Fraser and Mr. Samson were there, too. So the *Paragon* . . . was that the new—

"Kevin Gilmore! Am I glad to see you!" crowed Rev. Paton as he shook Kevin's hand. "We thought you were lost. No one knew what had happened to you!"

Kevin smiled and nodded to his old friends, then tried to slip away. If the missionaries knew, they might be angry with him for destroying the *Dayspring*.

"Not so fast, young man." The commodore grabbed his shoulder, then turned to the gathered missionaries. "You may not realize that this is the young man who saved your ship from further service in the slave trade. We have McNeil and his men in custody, and we'll soon catch Williams. However, they'd be gone by now if this lad hadn't scuttled the *Dayspring* in one of the bravest actions I've ever heard of. I'd be proud to have him under my command."

Captain Fraser's mouth dropped open. "You sank the *Dayspring*?"

But when the story came out, Captain Fraser stepped forward and shook Kevin's hand. John Paton, however, gave him a big hug. "Kevin, once we heard what those traders were doing with the *Dayspring*, we prayed night and day with many tears that God would put an end to it. You were our answer. It is better that our white-winged ship passed away than suffer such pollution and live on in disgrace! Thank you, lad." The missionary looked closely at Kevin. "By the way, it sounds like you must have found your source of courage."

All Kevin could do was nod his head and look down at the ground.

"Oh," said the commodore, "I have more news. Your mission board in Australia sends word that the *Paragon*"—he pointed at the three-masted ship in the bay—"which Captain Fraser chartered temporarily to bring you all here, has now been purchased to replace the *Dayspring*. Furthermore, its name has been officially changed and registered as the

Dayspring II so that everyone will recognize it as the true missionary ship."

While everyone celebrated the good news, Captain Fraser tapped Kevin's arm. "Would you like a berth on the *Dayspring II*? Not as a cabin boy, either. How about 'able seaman' on God's missionary ship to the islands?"

Kevin grinned but couldn't speak. Gratefulness flooded his whole being. He'd found the purpose for his life. And now he knew God *would* protect him until it was "his time." Maybe someday . . . someday he'd even become a captain of a ship that would serve missionaries.

More About John G. Paton

John Paton quit school as a young boy because of a cruel schoolmaster. But he was determined to become a missionary, so he studied at home.

Born into a fine Christian home in Dumfries, Scotland, in 1824, John saved enough by the time he was twelve to pay for six weeks of private schooling. He continued to work his way through school, university, divinity school, and medical training. Finally, at the age of thirty-four, he was ordained by the Presbyterian Church of Scotland and commissioned as a missionary to the South Sea Islands.

On November 5, 1858, John and his new wife, Mary Ann, arrived on Tanna in the New Hebrides, a group of eighty islands now known as Vanuatu, about fifteen hundred miles northeast of Australia.

Other missionaries had established a solid work on Anatom, a southern island in the New Hebrides, and several of their converts accompanied the Patons north to Tanna. At first the Patons felt overwhelmed by the warring cannibals of Tanna. Then they realized that the Christians from Anatom had been just as savage only a few years earlier.

The Tannese people worshiped and feared many idols and had no concept of a loving God. Witches and wizards in each village cast spells they claimed controlled life and death. They stirred up the people to drive out the missionaries.

Warfare between tribes increased, with some of the worst fighting happening right outside the Patons' house.

Three months after arriving on Tanna, Mary Ann Paton gave birth to their son, Peter, but she became sick with fever and died on March 3. Their son also died from fever less than three weeks later. Paton was so shaken by these tragedies that he could hardly continue, but God sustained him.

Not long after this, white traders—who also hated missionaries because they discouraged the natives from buying rum and muskets—deliberately sent three sick sailors among the people to spread measles, knowing that the witch doctors would blame Paton. The epidemic killed a third of the people, and the survivors sought revenge.

Two local chiefs protected Paton for a time, but that only increased the intertribal warfare. Soon Paton was running for his life, protected for a while by one chief, only to be chased by the same tribe the next day. He almost certainly would have been killed and probably eaten if a passing ship had not rescued him.

He had been on Tanna less than four years.

John then spent nearly two years speaking to churches in Australia and Scotland, raising financial support and recruiting more missionaries. One of those recruits, Margaret Whitecross, married and later returned with John to the islands.

One of Paton's objectives was to build a ship dedicated to serving the missionaries of the South Sea Islands. They needed dependable support, regular supplies, and on occasion—such as Paton had experienced—rescuing. Also, he found it unsatisfactory to rely on the unpredictable arrival of trading vessels for these services. Plus, why encourage visits by those unscrupulous traders with their immoral and abusive crew members?

Paton raised the money for the ship by selling "shares" for a few cents each to thousands of Sunday school children as well as adults in Australia and Scotland. It was a great success, and the *Dayspring* was built in Nova Scotia. In 1865 it delivered John Paton, his new wife and son, and several other missionaries to the South Sea Islands. A hurricane wrecked the *Dayspring* in 1873, but French slavers salvaged her for a brief time. This greatly distressed Paton because the natives were inclined to welcome her, not realizing that the traders aboard were likely to kidnap them as slaves. A second storm destroyed her for good. Later a *Dayspring II,* and finally a *Dayspring III,* served the island missionaries.

Upon returning to the islands, John longed to settle again on Tanna, but the mission board assigned the Patons to Aniwa a few miles east. Superstitions on Aniwa were just as godless, but possibly because the island was smaller, there was less warfare and cannibalism. As the Patons learned the language, they slowly gained the people's confidence and were able to present the Gospel until nearly everyone on the island became a Christian.

In his later years, Paton traveled widely on behalf of missions, but he always returned to his home on Aniwa until old age and failing health forced him to leave the island permanently in 1904. Though he was very sad to go, he rejoiced that the people now lived in peace and faithfully worshiped God.

He died January 28, 1907.

For Further Reading

Bell, Ralph. *John G. Paton.* Butler, Indiana: Higley Press, 1957.

Cromarty, Jim. *King of the Cannibals.* Durham, England: Evangelical Press, 1997.

Paton, John G. *John G. Paton—Missionary to the New Hebrides.* London: Hodder and Stroughton, 1891. The popular edition, "complete in one volume."

Paton, Margaret Whitecross. *Letters and Sketches From the New Hebrides.* London: Hodder and Stoughton, 1896.

Unseth, Benjamin. *John Paton.* Minneapolis: Bethany House Publishers, 1996.